BETTER SELVES

A COLLECTION OF SF&F STORIES

SONIA ORIN LYRIS

AFTERWORD BY
BARRY N. MALZBERG

KNOTTED ROAD PRESS

Better Selves
A Collection of SF&F Stories
Sonia Orin Lyris
Copyright © 2022 Sonia Orin Lyris
All rights reserved
Published by Knotted Road Press
www.KnottedRoadPress.com

ISBN: 978-1-64470-299-4

Cover art:
Photo 105619442 © Altaoosthuizen | Dreamstime.com

Interior design copyright © 2022 Knotted Road Press

It's True. Reviews Help.

If you like this collection, please consider giving it a rating. Same for any book and author: if you like the work, please say so. A note, a good review —these things can make a difference.

Want more?

I announce new projects on my Facebook feed.

http://facebook.com/authorlyris

You can also sign up for my newsletter.

https://lyris.org/subscribe/

Seeking the Singularity © 2022 by Barry N. Malzberg

The Angels' Share originally published in *Asimov's Science Fiction Magazine*, December 1996.

CONTENTS

INTRODUCTION

What happens when we fail ourselves? When we look in the mirror and don't like what we see?

If life is a series of on-stage performances in which we discover our lines, if we never know if we're the star or the walk-on, then who is that creature in the mirror?

We mean well, these selves we try so hard to be. We do our best. Sometimes we slip. Sometimes we fall.

Then what?

These five SF&F stories are explorations of the self, who we are when we're not our best, and how we can—at least sometimes—find our way back to the better part of ourselves.

THE ANGEL'S SHARE

A good single malt whiskey is aged in a cask for many years. Could be ten years, twenty, or more. Every one of those years, the whiskey loses a percent and a half of itself to evaporation. Distillers call this the *angel's share*.

The day I learned this was the day I started writing this story.

Twenty-three years after publication, I received an email from Barry N. Malzberg, who had just come across the story in his attic. He wrote:

"'The Angels' Share' is astonishing. You're a major talent. The unsparing integrity of this story does not give an inch."

He assured me that the story had aged well.

Have a sip.

First published in *Asimov's Science Fiction Magazine*, December 1996.

PHANTOM WATCHED Owl from the far end of the pool. The other man stood on the diving board, his wet, coffee-colored skin accenting his toned, muscular body. Owl bounced a little, testing the spring of the board.

Even if Owl had ever been as good a diver as he claimed, it would have to have been at least fifty years ago, long before the recent fall that broke Owl's fragile hip, forcing the old man to surgery and rehab. However good Owl might have been then, it was long ago, when Owl had been in his own body.

So Phantom watched from the other end of the pool.

Owl was grinning in obvious pleasure. Phantom understood: the other man had only been here a week, and Phantom knew well how the sudden lack of pain could make you feel reborn.

The board went down deep a few times, then snapped up as Owl launched himself into the air, tucked into a ball, and spun above the pool. At the last moment he uncurled and sliced into the water.

In a moment, a fuzzy black head popped up next to Phantom.

"God, this is wonderful," Owl said, shaking the water from his head.

Phantom chuckled. "Almost as good as the original, eh?"

Owl's smile faded. "No."

"It never is," Phantom said softly.

It was a sunny day in Paradise. But then, this near the equator, the weather was usually warm and often sunny. They paid for the weather, like they paid for the olympic-size swimming pool, tennis courts, world-class chefs, and the razor wire atop the high walls.

It was all part of the Paradise package, and the package cost. But then, three months in a young, handsome athletic body was bound to be pricey. Three months of relief while someone else took over the rehab of your broken body. It didn't come cheap.

"This your first time?" Phantom asked Owl.

Owl nodded. "And you?"

"I was here last year."

"Huh." Owl was obviously impressed. Body swaps were limited to one a year, if you could afford it.

The year limit was for the same reason that the swap started to deteriorate after three months; too much of having another consciousness mapped onto your brain and the brain started to abandon connections. Phantom knew about it; his company had pursued its own research and he had seen the tests on monkeys. By five months the monkeys were unable to feed themselves, and when attempts were made to transfer the original consciousness back, the monkeys threw themselves at the bars of the cages until they smashed their heads into bloody unconsciousness.

The fact was that a single trip to Paradise cost more than most people would see in a lifetime. Wealth alone was not enough to get you in; Paradise only provided transfers to those who would medically benefit, and whose original bodies were likely to survive the three months.

"So," Owl said, drawing out the question with a wave of his hand, "what brings you to Paradise?"

"Chemotherapy," Phantom said, smiling hard into Owl's questioning face.

"Ah," Owl said, looking down.

"Probably be my last visit," Phantom added, still smiling. "Too bad it's only three months, eh?"

Owl gave Phantom a quick, sharp glance which Phantom pointedly ignored.

"There." Phantom pointed at two women. In a single swift movement that he could never have done in his own body, even when he was this young, Phantom put his hands on the edge of the pool and lifted himself out. Owl followed him up and they stood together like a couple of dripping Adonises.

The two women had just stepped out of the offices. They stood on the tiled path, blinking in the hot sun.

"New," Phantom said softly to Owl.

The women walked down the path, each carrying a suitcase with the Paradise logo, which would be filled with the clothes the host had picked out before the body swap.

"New," Owl echoed with a sly grin. "You thinking of making a friend or two, Phantom?"

The women were exquisite, of course. With the wealth that came through Paradise, Paradise hosts had to be the best. That, after all, was part of the draw.

The first woman was dark haired, and dark eyed, an olive green silk dress flattering her slender figure. She had an exotic look, probably due to an Asian grandparent. She walked lightly, as though she was afraid she might break. Probably recovering from an accident. The second woman was small and compact, muscled like a swimmer. She had large blue eyes and a mane of hair the color of orange flame that fell past the shoulders of her yellow sun dress.

Phantom chuckled. "Carrot Top's a fatty."

There were a lot of reasons to come to Paradise, but basically it was about having someone else do your dirty work for you. You hired a host to do rehab after an accident, or take the painful chemo treatments that were your last stab at life. Or maybe you hired someone to repair the damage you had done to yourself.

"You mean she's here to lose weight?" Owl laughed. "How can you tell?"

"I'm a businessman, Owl. You don't build a successful business on products, you build it on people. I've spent a lot of years watching people. And my business is very successful."

The two women had probably gone through the transfer process last night. They would have already slept in their new bodies one evening and this morning white-clad angels—the Paradise staff—would lead them through two hours of 'get acquainted' exercises. The new body would have none of the problems of the old, so it didn't take long to get comfortable enough in the new body so it felt like you belonged there.

Going back, of course, was a bitch.

Paradise clients didn't get a choice about that, though. The three month limit wasn't just the way the contract was worded; the technology could not make the transfer last longer. After three months the transfer started to deteriorate as both host and client bodies "rejected" the new brain mapping, and hence the consciousness that inhabited the body. Another month without returning both inhabitants to their original bodies and both client and host would be vegetables.

When faced with that eventuality, most people would willingly—if reluctantly—return to their own bodies. Paradise depended on it.

"Look at the way Carrot Top moves," Phantom said to Owl. "Her half-shuffle. Hesitation in each step. She's used to being in a much larger body. Two hundred pounds, at least. It'll take her longer to adjust to the host body because of her self-image. I bet she puts twenty pounds on that body before she leaves Paradise."

"What a way to diet."

"What a goddamn waste," Phantom said. "Her host will starve and exercise for three months, then Carrot will go and put all the fat right back on again."

"Don't have much faith in human nature, do you?"

"Just enough faith, Owl."

Phantom grabbed a towel from a pile and started to dry his legs off. The sight of his leg momentarily took him by surprise. Even after four weeks in Paradise, he was still startled when he saw a piece of his body, young and healthy.

Mirrors were spare here. Paradise didn't want to encourage clients to become too attached to their host bodies. At the same time, clients paid for the privilege of being perfect, even if just for three months, so by the pool there were mirrors.

Phantom admired his image. The angels matched coloring between host and client, but the sandy brown hair and pale green eyes were all that his original body had in common with his host's body. His host was good-looking enough to be a model or an actor. Instead he rented his body to wealthy men with damaged bodies.

Phantom didn't envy his host right now. The fellow would be enduring the worst of the course of chemotherapy Phantom's body was due to receive this time around.

Of course, his host only had to rent his body out a few times, do his part to rehab the client, and he could retire in luxurious comfort. Unpleasant as a host's job might be, there was no shortage of hosts.

Or clients.

Phantom chuckled. "Yes," he said to Owl as the women passed by, "a new friend might be just the thing."

PHANTOM FOLLOWED THE RED-HEADED WOMAN. He was careful not to be obvious, but the effort was probably wasted. She seemed dazed.

Newcomers often were. The shock of being in a new body, one that was not sick, or—in this case—not fat, was startling.

He watched her walk to her room, noted the number, and went back to his own. He showered, and changed into a T-shirt, jeans and sandals and returned to the red-head's room.

She would probably still be inside, wrapped in uncertainty about venturing out of her room. He knocked. After a moment she opened the door.

"Welcome to Paradise," Phantom said. "May I come in?"

She looked startled and stepped back.

Good looks, Phantom had discovered, were much better than lock picks. She clearly was not used to handsome men taking an interest in her. He stepped inside, shut the door behind him, and gave her a winning smile.

"Who are you?" she asked.

"The welcoming committee. You can call me Phantom."

He stepped up very close to her and touched her face very lightly, tracing the line of her jaw. She stood there, frozen.

"Phantom is just my nickname," he continued. "Most people use nicknames to protect their privacy while they're in Paradise. And I've got a nickname for you. Carrot Top, for that amazing hair."

"I don't think we're supposed to be..." she said, her hands hanging limply at her sides, her face tight with uncertainty—and something else. Hope, it looked like.

"You're a good girl, aren't you." Phantom continued to outline her face, moving to her ears. "The angels told you no sex and you believed them."

She inhaled. Soft, but he heard it.

"Well, let me tell you something else, Carrot." He pulled his hand away from her face suddenly, to get all of her attention. It worked; her eyes focused on him and she caught her breath.

"These bodies they gave us," he said, "they're disease free.

No venereal diseases. All the men are sterile. So you see, they say 'no', but they really mean 'have fun'."

He put his hands on her shoulders. Her muscles relaxed a little under his fingers, telling him that her instinct was not to resist. He her pushed gently toward the bed and she took a clumsy step backward.

"So let's have some fun," he said.

Her hands floated up between them as though they were looking in vain for something to push against.

"No," she said. "I—"

He pulled his hands back. "You want me to stop, Carrot?"

"I—" she trailed off.

"I'll stop if you like," he said, smiling. "I'll leave. Is that what you want? Just say so."

Her eyes betrayed a mix of emotions, a warring of insecurities.

"Well?"

He waited until it was clear she would not speak.

"I'll bet you're a virgin, too."

Her eyes widened, just enough. He chuckled.

"Thought so."

Phantom pressed her back again. Her legs bumped the edge of the bed and he pushed her on her back, carefully falling on top of her, his arms holding himself off her. She crossed her arms.

"Please," she said from under him, her voice tight. "I don't want—"

"You don't know what you want. Not yet." He pulled her arms away from her breasts, pressed them to her sides, caught her gaze. "You don't know because you've never had it. Just a fat, shy girl, all your short life. Now you've got this perfect body with a perfect man on top of you and you don't know what to do or what to feel."

He'd hit home; her face twisted as she tried not to cry.

"Confused, but not irredeemably so," he said gently. He brought his face close and brushed her lips with his. Her body tensed. "You're a stunning beauty, you know."

On her face desire struggled with fear. For a moment fear took over as she tried to pull away, but she was easy to hold. She had no idea how strong her new body was, still thought of herself as weak. Proof of his greater strength was all she needed to convince her to stop struggling.

He grabbed a large handful of her thick, red hair and twisted her head to the side, exposing her white neck, stroking the skin there with his lips, nibbling at the softest spots. His other hand snaked over the top of her low-cut dress, traveling along her soft breasts and playing with her nipples, making them hard. His hand came out, went down between her legs, fingers slipping under her underwear.

She was breathing hard. When he found what he was searching for she whimpered.

"Please," she whispered.

"Please yes, or please no? Which is it?" He pushed a finger inside her to feel her wetness. "You don't want it, eh? Your body says you're a liar, Carrot."

She did not fight him now as he took off her clothes, but lay there, tense and unmoving, watching him as he took off his own.

He marveled at bright red hair against flawless white skin, at the thin red tracks his nails left on her flat, hard stomach. Spreading her legs, he tasted her. She made a sound halfway between a moan and a sob.

He pulled himself up on top of her again. When he plunged into her she gave a small cry that mingled with his moan. As he moved, her whimpers softened.

"I've had dozens like you," he whispered into her ear, breathing hard. "You can lie to yourself, but your body can't lie to me." He pushed himself deep in again, and she inhaled. "How does it feel, to be wanted? To be hungered for? Tell me you don't like it and I'll stop."

She blinked up at him, her blue eyes wet, tears like jewels on her copper lashes.

Phantom kissed her again, hard and deep, felt her hesitant response. Then it grabbed him completely, his twenty year old body doing easily what his real body, old and infested with cancer, no longer could. He felt himself thrown to the top of a high, fiery peak and hurled over the summit.

He lay on her, catching his breath, swimming in sweetness. After a while he pulled out, brushed her cheek with his fingertips, and stood, marveling at the drive and energy his new body had.

"How about a drink, Carrot?" he asked.

She lay curled up on the bed.

"The angels like us to treat our host bodies real nice, so the bar's only open for two hours. Now's our chance." He pulled on his pants and shirt.

He sat down on the bed next to her, stroking strands of flame-colored hair out of her face.

"This is life, little one. The heat of the chase, the passion of flesh—my flesh, your flesh—" She put a hand up to stop his touch.

He grabbed her hand. "All the things you never knew about," he said. "Now's your chance. If you don't run with it now, you'll be back in your prison of flesh before you know it. Do you think it will make that much difference, losing a few pounds?" He shook his head. "The difference is in you."

She shut her eyes and turned away. He grabbed a fistful of her hair, forced her to face him.

Her eyes opened wide, a startling blue, like the sky over Paradise.

"How old are you?" She didn't answer so he shook her head a little.

"Twenty-two," she whispered.

"Well, I'm eighty-seven. So when I talk, you'd do well to listen. Three months in Paradise isn't a lot, but it might be enough for you to find out some things about yourself. To find something to fill yourself with besides food. Stop living in a shell, Carrot. Go take some chances. Have some fun."

She looked like she might cry again.

"I know," he said gently. "You hate me for telling you the truth. Hate me, then. But think about my words. Paradise is your chance. And right now there isn't long left for that drink."

After a minute of silence he got up and left. As he closed the door behind him he heard her begin to sob.

TORCHES LIT the Paradise bar as the tropical sunlight faded. The blinds had been rolled up to let in the warm night air. The only permanent resident of Paradise, a large green parrot by the door, greeted Phantom with his usual "come right in and have a drink."

"You're looking younger every year, Percy," Phantom said to the bird. The bird cocked his head and responded, "Happy, happy, Paradise."

Phantom chuckled and looked around. The bar was crowded, as always. Owl sat in a far corner with a half dozen other people, most of them women.

Phantom's arrangement with Owl had been made back in the real world, when Owl was considering coming to Paradise to rehab his hip. Aside from the man's business background and willingness to spend a lot of money on new youth, Phantom knew little about him. That was all right;

Owl knew nothing at all about Phantom. Owl's reputation in the business world said he knew how to keep his mouth shut. Phantom hoped he would remember.

Phantom's eyes fell on the other new woman, the dark haired one. She sat alone, and Phantom's eyes widened in surprise at his good luck. He walked over to her table.

"Welcome to Paradise," he said. "You should have company on your first night here. May I join you?"

"Sure," she said. "Have a seat." He did.

She was dressed in silk again, a simple black dress that she wore with the slightly awkward posture of the newly arrived. She was beautiful, like everyone in Paradise, but to Phantom's eyes she stood out. Her expression was one one of openness, as if she had yet to make up her mind about the things around her. She took a sip of her drink and looked long at him.

"What?" he asked, feigning a touch of self-conscious uncertainty. He looked down at himself as if to check his clothes.

She shook her head. "I was just wondering how you could tell I was new."

"I saw you and Carrot Top together as you walked out of the offices this morning. The uncertain look, the suitcase—a dead giveaway."

"Ah."

She poked at the ice in her drink with a long, perfectly shaped nail.

"What should I call you?" he asked.

"My name is Celeste."

"I'm Phantom," he said. He raised a finger to signal a waiter.

"I'll have—whatever she's having," he told the waiter.

"Scotch," she said.

"Scotch," he repeated. "Glenlivet," he added.

"The good stuff," she said.

"The best."

The waiter returned a few moments later with Phantom's drink.

He took a sip. "I used to make my living overseeing production of this stuff," he said.

"You don't say."

"Oh, but it's true. People will say all sorts of things here in Paradise. They feel renewed, they think they can be anyone, and no one can check. But I have no need to impress you with little things like that."

She gave him an amused smile.

"Don't believe me?" He sat back. "Did you know that a good single malt whiskey has to age at least ten years?"

She shook her head.

"As it ages, about a percent and a half of it evaporates every year. The Scots call this 'the angels' share.'"

Celeste laughed once. Softly, charmingly. Now she believed him. Or she didn't care.

"Here in Paradise," Phantom went on, smiling, "the angels always get their share. So we have to take what we can in the short time we have."

"I suppose you had something specific in mind."

"You might say that."

He put his hand on top of hers, stroked her fingers lightly.

She looked at his hand, her smile vanishing.

"What do you think you're doing?"

"Touching you," he said, keeping his eyes on her. "Wanting to touch you more."

"Yes, I know," she said. "I look great. The image in the mirror stuns me, too. But we've just met and you're moving way too fast." She pulled her hand back away from his.

"We have to move fast here. Time is something we don't

have a lot of." He walked his fingers toward her on the table like a spider. "I've been here over a month already."

"I see. Only two months left to play." She brought her palm down slowly on his fingers, flattening his hand against the table under hers. "So you run around Paradise, screwing gorgeous women. Must be a hard life."

"I'm not complaining," Phantom said. "Nothing like a twenty-something year old body to help clarify your priorities."

She looked at him knowingly. "But you're not twenty-something, are you. Much older, I'd guess."

He nodded.

"An old man in a young man's body," she said. "What a killer combination. All the confidence and experience of age mixed with physical youth and virility. You must clean up."

Phantom could not keep himself from grinning. "You should find out."

She laughed once and moved her hand over his caressingly.

"Is it hard to leave here?"

His smile dimmed. "You forget the pain when you're here. You forget a lot of things. Then you go back. It's like going to prison."

Her focus was distant. "It's odd, thinking of how my host's mind is in my real body now, trying to rehab my legs after the accident."

He gave her an interested, questioning look. "I won't pry."

She shrugged.

"A semi had my car for lunch and my legs for dessert." Her lips twitched, trying for a smile. "So now I pay a stranger to take my pain and do my work. Still, it feels strange, having someone else suffer for me."

"Nothing to feel bad about. Your host is getting paid," Phantom said. "Plenty."

"And in three months she'll be back in this fabulous body and I'll never walk again."

"So enjoy those legs while you've got them."

"If we could stay here longer..."

"Wouldn't that be nice."

Her voice got quiet. "You know, I heard someone at the bar say there's a chemical that can counter the rejection process. Let you stay longer than three months."

Phantom laughed. "That rumor and Percy the parrot are the only two things that never leave Paradise."

Celeste looked disappointed. "You're sure?"

"Even if there was a way to prevent a body from rejecting a transferred consciousness—" he shrugged. "You'd still have a handful of problems. A hell of a time finding a host, for one. Three months, for big bucks, yes. But a lifetime? You couldn't pay anyone enough."

"I suppose that's true."

"You know, there's another rumor going around. About an angel under cover."

"Really? What for?"

He shrugged. "Maybe the angels think someone really has an anti-rejection drug and they're checking around. 'Celeste'—'of heaven'. Am I right?"

"It was my aunt's name."

He watched her for a long moment. Her brows drew together, then her nostrils flared once.

"Maybe I'm an angel under cover, is that what you're saying?"

"No, I'm just being paranoid. They keep us under very tight tabs here. I get kind of tired of it, is all. I'm sorry."

"Celeste really is my name. You could check the files. I'd be happy to authorize it."

He smiled at her, a mix of admiration and amused skepticism.

"I'm serious," she said.

"I know you are. But records can be doctored."

"Gods above, Phantom. If I were an angel, would I choose such an obvious name? Some people here use their real names, you know. Like me."

Phantom had learned, many years ago and in the hardest possible way, that there was no sure way to spot a liar. He had also learned that never to trust is never to win.

"I believe you," he said. "No under cover angels, and no anti-rejection drug."

She sighed. "So that's how it is. Three months in Paradise and then back to hell."

He shrugged. "Three months or a hundred years." He moved his chair closer to hers. "You still have to make the moments count."

Celeste regarded him a moment, then nodded.

"Come to my room, Celeste."

"You're very good at this."

"Wait until you see what I'm really good at."

He could tell that she hadn't planned to smile at that, but couldn't help it. She was charmed. He took her hand and stood, drawing her up. She put her arm through his, and together they walked out.

"SO," Owl asked Phantom over breakfast, "how was it?"

"How was what?" Phantom asked. He was distracted, looking around the dining room for Celeste.

Owl nodded at another table.

"There. Chowing down. Your Carrot Top."

Phantom looked at the red head, grinned. "Tasty. The

host body isn't, of course, but—" he tapped his head, "up here she's all cherry. Or was."

"You stud," Owl said, half mockingly, half admiringly.

Phantom looked around the room again for a dark head of hair.

"She's packing it away," Owl said, still staring at the red-head. "You were right."

"Of course. You don't change a person by changing their body. Her host will take off some fat and then spend another three months taking off what Carrot Top put on her body while she was away. When Carrot gets back, she'll eat herself back to where she was in no time flat, having wasted the entire three months here."

Owl chuckled. "You don't have much faith in human nature, do you."

"Plenty of faith. I've seen it before. I didn't make myself rich by underestimating human stupidity."

"One of these days I'd like to know just what kind of business you're in."

Phantom chuckled. "Retired."

"Sure," Owl said skeptically, then looked back at the red-haired woman. "Twenty pounds in three months, you say. I'd bet on the red-head. I think she'll find other things to do in Paradise besides eating. I think she'll change."

"I'd take that bet for real money and you'd lose," Phantom said. "It's a shame we won't be around to find out."

Owl's dark eyes were suddenly on him. "When do we leave?"

Phantom lowered his voice. "Tonight, 11pm, at the east end of Paradise, where there's a dock gate. No extra clothes, don't look like you're packing to leave. And don't be late."

"The drug—are you sure—"

Phantom cut him off with a sharp hand gesture. "You either trust me or you don't."

He and Owl locked gazes a moment, then Owl nodded.

A dark haired woman walked into the room, sat down at a table.

"Aha. Excuse me," Phantom said, standing.

At another table, another man stood, tall, muscular, and blond. He reached out and grabbed the collar of the shorter, dark haired man with him, and yanked him to his feet. The smaller man put one hand on the arm holding his collar, the other on the elbow, and quickly dropped. There was a dull crack and the taller man howled. Other men surrounded the two, and in moments it turned into a brawl, complete with curses and the sound of fists hitting flesh.

Phantom walked around the edge of the room, making his way toward Celeste. Everyone was standing now, most backing away from the fight or going toward it. It wouldn't take long for the bouncer-sized white clad angels to come and break it up.

Phantom passed behind the red head. He stepped up to her, put his mouth by her ear.

"Morning, Carrot dear," he whispered. She jumped, turned, backed a step away from him, bumping into someone else who glared then looked back at the fight. "Don't worry," Phantom said, nodding at the brawl. "Men tend to be a little violent at this age, and most of them don't know how to deal with being strong, good looking, and young all at once. Now, us older men, even in young bodies, we know how to control our temper."

"But not your—" she said, then flushed.

"But not our dicks?" He grinned. "Want to do it again tonight? Test my control some more?"

Her eyes widened and she shook her head. "I should report you."

He laughed. "But you won't. You keep saying 'no', Carrot

Top, and someone's going to believe you. It isn't really what you want. Is it?"

He stared at her until she looked away, then he stepped past her, chuckling, trailing his fingers across her breast. She sniffed and pulled away, but it took her a moment too long.

He found Celeste, standing by the door, watching the scuffle. He admired her for a moment before stepping close and taking her hand.

"You look great," he said softly.

"So do you."

"I'd better. I paid plenty for this flesh."

"Are you free tonight?" she asked.

He shook his head wistfully, almost regretting his appointment with his own future.

"Ah," she said, disappointed but still smiling. "Another date?"

"Not that sort. I think you've ruined me for sex with anyone else. Last night was definitely a high water mark."

"Bet you say that to all the girls."

"Yes, but this time I mean it."

She laughed, shrugged. "Easy come, easy go."

"No, not with you. I mean—" He stepped up close to her, caressed her cheek. What was there about her? "Damn."

"Excuse me?"

"Damn my appointment. Will you give me your real name, so I can look you up when we get back to our real bodies?"

"Will you give me yours?"

He snorted and shook his head. They grinned at each other.

"Then how about tomorrow night?" she asked.

"I'd like to," he said. Except that he wouldn't be here tomorrow and he couldn't tell her that. "Look for me. We'll set something up."

The thought of her wandering around Paradise looking for him after he was gone was a bittersweet image that tugged at him.

"All right," she said with a warm smile. He echoed her smile, the pretense harder than it should have been.

PHANTOM KNEW Joe from the real world, from years ago, had employed him before as a body guard. Now Joe was on the other side of the dock's locked gate, in the darkness, his penlight illuminating the card-lock that separated Phantom and Owl from Joe and his boat. Phantom didn't know the details of how Joe had managed to get the card key and combination, but it didn't matter who had been bribed or pressured to reveal the information. It only mattered that Joe had it, and could open the gate that would take Owl and Phantom to freedom and new lives.

A bright, focused beam brushed nearby tree tops then vanished.

"We have company," Owl said softly. Joe, about to open the lock, reached instead for his gun. The light passed again, closer, toward the top of the tall gate.

"Damn," Phantom whispered. "Joe, we've got to cancel." At Owl, he hissed, "Run. I'll catch up with you later." Owl took off at a quiet jog through the brush.

"Skip to next rendezvous," Phantom told Joe, referring to to a prearranged time that only they two knew.

"You've got a rat," Joe whispered back.

"Could be an accidental pass-by, no?"

"No. I know Paradise. There shouldn't be anyone here now. If it's a client on the other end of that beam, then it's a fluke, but if it's an angel, you've got a rat on your ship and I don't want it on mine."

Phantom exhaled his frustration. There was a bitter taste in his mouth and the light was coming back. "All right," he told Joe. "Meet next time."

Phantom took off in the direction that Owl had gone. He followed the light back through the trees until he saw a flash of angel white.

There was only one person it could be. He was on his way to Owl's room when he changed his mind and his direction. Owl could wait. He knocked on Celeste's door.

The door opened and she stood there blinking, as if she had just been woken. He stepped inside, shut the door behind him.

"My date canceled," he said. It felt good to see her again. Very good. Somewhere inside he was almost glad for the failed escape. That was not a good reaction; he had to be careful.

"I was asleep."

"Sorry. Want some company?"

"Oh, Phantom, I'm tired, not really up for—" she grinned. "A repeat of last night. Not just yet."

He stared at her a moment, taken with her beauty. He sat down on the bed next to her.

"How about if I just stay here with you? Just sleep here next to you?"

"Careful, you'll make me feel special."

He nodded soberly. "Good. So, may I stay?"

She looked at him curiously. "I know your type, Phantom; you manipulate, you get people to dance to your music. What are you doing here with me?"

It was a good question. He wasn't sure.

"Let's just say that I like you. I'd like to get to know you better."

She grinned. "Yeah, me too. Guess it doesn't make any

more sense to you than it does it me. But we've a month to figure it out. And honestly, right now I'm really tired."

He shook his head. "I don't have a month. I'm going back early."

"Early?" She frowned. "But I thought you said——"

"I know. Something's come up with my treatment. They can't risk the host body, so I have to go back."

"Oh my God," she said, sitting down on the bed. "When I get back, I'll come see you. Tell me your real name, Phantom. I'll give you my last name, too."

"I can't."

"Why not? I thought you wanted to see me again."

"I do. Very much. More than I can explain. But——Celeste, I'm terminal. My original body can't even support much in the way of clear thought any more. Even if I survive the three months of treatment——I don't want you to see me like that. Better for you to remember me like this."

She shook her head. "That's stupid."

"Yes, but I'm a proud man. A proud old man, and don't you forget it. You're——what?——in your early forties?"

"Yes. You're good."

"Thanks. I'm pushing ninety, Celeste. A sick, frail, dying old man. You don't need that."

"Don't tell me what I need."

"All right, then I'll tell you what I need. I need to know that you last saw me like this. Healthy. Alive. In love with you."

"Don't give me that crap," she said, but she was smiling.

"All right," he said seriously. "No crap. I'm in love with you."

She lost her smile. "When do you leave?"

"Tomorrow night. That gives us——" He inhaled sharply. "tonight, and all of tomorrow."

"Talk about whirlwind love affairs..."

He stroked her cheek. "Still tired?"

She shook her head. Tears welled up in her eyes, fell over the brim, trailed down her face. She moved her head against his fingertips.

"Damn it, Phantom. This isn't the way it's supposed to happen."

"I know. I'm sorry."

"So," she said softly, her voice rough, "let's make some moments count, shall we?"

"Let's."

HE STAYED with her that night and the next day, not leaving the room. When they got hungry, they sent out for food. They talked about everything, his business, her family—everything except death and Paradise.

He kept telling himself to be careful, but at the last moment he could not seem to stop himself; he told her about the boat, the trip, and the drug.

He sat on the edge of the bed, took her hand.

"Come with me, Celeste."

She frowned. "But what about the host body?"

"The host stays in my old body."

"Your old body is dying, you said."

He gave her a quick smile. "I exaggerated a bit. I've got cancer, but they still consider it treatable or I wouldn't be here. Thing is, I know better. I can feel it in my bones, that my body is dying, and dying fast." He shrugged. "I'm ninety, what do you expect?"

"Then—the host will die, too?"

"He's got the same chance I had."

"And that's not much."

"It's me or him. Sometimes you have to give something to get something else."

"And it's easier to give up someone else's body."

"Easier than my own, that's for sure."

She pulled her hand out of his, looked away. "The angels' share."

"Excuse me?"

"What you lose, year after year of life, that makes you so—concentrated."

"And that is?"

"Your morals."

He exhaled. "Celeste, I don't have time for this. Come with me. I know it's not as much of a benefit for you, you being only forty, but it's twenty years more of life for you, too, and you'd keep this body, complete with working legs."

"Tempting. But—I couldn't live with myself if I did that. To trap someone else in my broken body...?"

He glanced at his watch. "Two minutes until I walk out that door. I have to go or I'll die. Come with me, Celeste."

"No, stay with me. You can get better, if you really want to. And I don't care if you're ninety or a hundred, I love you and—"

He snorted. "I won't live out the year in my own body, no matter what I do. Not even that long, Celeste. And never mind sex. What would there be to love?"

"Phantom, this isn't right. You shouldn't do this."

"Celeste, I can't stay."

"Then go," she said very softly.

He swallowed, ignoring the pain in his head, and bent to kiss her mouth, but she turned away, tears in her eyes. He kissed her forehead instead and stared at her face for a long moment trying to fix it in his mind. What did she really looked like? When he shut the door behind him his stomach felt hollow, as if something had been torn out.

JOE SLIPPED a plastic card into the security box at the east gate and punched in the access code. It was a dark night, with pale starlight and a bit of moon brushing silver on Paradise's tropical trees. Phantom turned his back on Joe to watch the woods for lights, but he was thinking about Celeste.

He found himself turning over plans in his head, about sending someone back to get her even though he knew she wouldn't come. Perhaps once he was away from Paradise, once he had freed himself of the yoke of disease and imminent death, he would find she held less hold on his heart. He almost hoped so.

Owl was, he decided, the only one who could have given them away last time, so this time Phantom had neglected to invite him.

Phantom's eyes flickered everywhere. This was his chance to live again. If ever there was a time to be careful, it was now.

"We're clear," Joe whispered behind him as the gate clicked open. Joe stepped back, opening the gate. Phantom turned to follow.

He felt as much as saw the movement behind him. He whirled as a shadow broke away from the night's corners and became a figure with a gun.

"Phantom, don't," she said.

He glanced at the gun, snorted. "'Of heaven'," he said. "Well played, my angel."

"I won't say a thing, I swear it. Just leave the gate, and come back."

"And die? I don't think so." He stepped toward the open gate. Joe was backing silently to the boat.

"Don't, Phantom," she said, her voice a mix of command and plea.

"You won't shoot me, Celeste. This is a host body. Be a terrible shame to put holes in it."

"No holes," she said, "tranqs. Phantom, don't make me do this. If you go any further, I'll tranq you and take you in."

"Nice to have choices," he said, stopping. He brought his hands up on either side of his face, his palms facing her. He wiggled his fingers.

"See?" he asked.

"See what?"

The quiet pop came from Joe's direction, and Celeste gave a muffled yelp and dropped to her knee, clutching her upper arm, the gun dangling from her fingers.

One part of Phantom's mind marveled at how well simple distractions worked. It was one of the oldest tricks in the book. The other part of him chilled at the sight of Celeste crumpling, her arm dripping blood.

He closed, kicked her onto her back and dropped a knee on the forearm of her injured side. She struggled with him, cursing softly as he twisted the gun out of her trembling grip.

"Move it," Joe hissed. "The gate's going to sound an alarm if it's open another thirty seconds."

Phantom aimed Celeste's gun at her.

"Hope you were telling the truth, sweetheart," he whispered as he shot her in the leg.

"Now!" Joe hissed.

Phantom reached down, hefted the limp woman, and threw her over his shoulder.

"What the hell...?" Joe asked angrily.

"Let's go," Phantom told him. He stepped through the gate, and Joe slammed it shut behind.

Swearing softly, Joe jumped onto the boat and fired up

the engine. Phantom boarded and went below deck, grabbing on tight as the boat lurched away from the dock.

Then he took Celeste down below, laid her on a bunk, and went for the first aid kit.

———

PHANTOM WENT BELOW to check on Celeste. They were days out of Paradise now, passing a cluster of small islands. Her shoulder was healing nicely. She must have heard Joe and turned a split second before he shot, because Joe never aimed to wound and he usually didn't miss.

Injured and drugged she might be, but Phantom had used plenty of duct tape to keep her tied, with less emphasis on her comfort than on his. The pain killers had kept her under, so there were bedpans and water bottles littered around the bunk. Joe would have nothing to do with her, so Phantom silently handled it all. She'd seemed unconscious or asleep most of the time, though Phantom was sure he had seen her eyes open to slits once or twice while he wandered around below deck.

She was an angel, all right. Paradise could afford it, so there was every reason to believe she was the best, hired to come in as a client and search for the semi-mythical transfer drug. He stared at her face for a long moment, thought about hitting her, thought about kissing her.

He checked the bandages on her shoulder and felt her head for fever. She moved under his touch, just as she had when they made love together.

"Celeste," he said, stroking her cheek with the back of his fingers.

She opened her eyes, moaned.

"You know, I really should be very angry with you."

"I'm still alive," she said, with wonder. She moved a little, struggling against the duct tape, and winced at the pain in her shoulder.

"You sucker punched me," Phantom said.

"Then why is it my shoulder that hurts like hell?"

"Bad aim on Joe's part. You should be dead."

She sighed, a long exhale.

"I thought," he said with a wry grin, "I'd been had for the last time, many years ago."

"Once you're sure of that, you're the best kind of target."

He chuckled. "Ah, Celeste... Not your real name, I assume."

"No."

"And the body?"

She hesitated. "Born with it."

"Damn," he said admiringly. "You can't be over twenty-five, girl. You're good."

"Not good enough. Phantom—"

"You know my real name," he said, suddenly run dry of polite conversation. "Why not use it?"

She looked genuinely startled. "Because I know you as Phantom. That's who you are to me. And yes, I caught you off guard. Yes, I suckered you. But you know—it wasn't in my contract to seduce you."

"I thought I seduced you."

"You did."

He laughed in spite of himself. "You're quite good."

"Thank you," she said, then exhaled. "Gods above, Phantom, when you asked me to come with you, I almost said yes."

"Don't give me that."

"It's true. I could have given up pursuing you, told them you didn't have the drugs, and then taken on a new identity, just to be with you. I seriously considered it. But I couldn't—it just isn't right."

"You mean trying to stay alive?"

"At the cost of someone else's life."

"A moralizing angel. Charming. I didn't create the cancer, Celeste. I didn't choose to grow old and sick. I use what I have to get what I need, that's all."

"And the man whose body you inhabit now? What about him?"

"What about him? He made his choices. He chose to be a host. You play the game, you take your chances."

She shook her head. "No. I can't condone that—"

"I'm not asking you to. I've been fighting the angels all my life. They always wanted a share of the good stuff I had. Every year of my life they took a bit more. Sagging mid-line, hurting knees, bad stomach. But the greedy little bastards weren't happy with that, they had to make my cells insane, too." He smiled humorlessly. "Now I'm taking it all back."

"You don't see it, do you."

"Oh, I think I see it pretty clearly."

"It's not your body you lost, year by year."

"My morals, you already told me."

"Yes. You gave away a bit of your heart every year. You let them take the stuff that makes you the kind of person who can care about another person. Who can love."

"Love." He tried to feel nothing, failed. "With you, I loved, Celeste."

She nodded. "Yes. So they haven't gotten it all, not quite. Phantom," she said earnestly, "come back with me. I'll testify on your behalf. Give this man's body back. Show me what you can be, show me that you can care that much."

"Not a chance in hell. I'd die. You have no idea what it's like to live with this shit—the chemo, the operations, the pain, the loss of my mind—you, with your young body, your health—you've got a lot of goddamned nerve telling me what's moral."

She stared back at him, her expression suddenly hard. His hand on her arm was shaking. She had pissed him off, and fast. Almost as fast as she had intrigued him. Almost as fast as she had made him love her.

"What you're doing is wrong. Damn it, Phantom, look inside yourself and—"

"That's it. I'm done with this conversation."

"I'm not. Listen—"

"Shut up, Celeste."

"And if I don't? I can't just sit here quiet and let you do this."

"If you can't offer me anything but the advice that I kill myself then I'll throw you overboard."

There wasn't a touch of fear in her expression. Good training and youth made her fearless of death. Somehow it made her even more beautiful to him, and that fueled his anger.

The angels had taken enough already. Now they wanted to take his heart as well. He wouldn't give it to them.

"Then do it," she hissed. "I'll drown. And with me throw out the last bit of what makes you human. Live a life of shallow pleasure in another man's body, while he dies an agonizing death in yours."

"Exactly what I had in mind."

"Then you'd better toss me over, because I'm not going to stop telling you what I think of you."

He squeezed her arm tightly. She didn't seem to notice.

"Don't challenge me, Celeste."

"Too much for you? Show me what you're made of, Phantom. I'm tied up. What a challenge for you to toss me in the drink. Another death on your hands, but so what? You've already done so much to preserve your own life. What's a little more?"

He gripped her arm harder.

"Don't."

"Or turn this boat back to Paradise. I'm not going to let you off, Phantom. I care too much about you to shut up."

"You can't keep your mouth shut, and I don't care to listen. One of us is going to lose."

Her voice became suddenly impassioned, pleading. "Phantom, come back with me. Give yourself up. Do what's right."

He grabbed her arms, hauled her out of the bed, and she howled and struggled, tearing open the bandage on her arm. Holding her under his arms like a sack of potatoes, something he would never be able to do in his original body, he walked up the steps to the deck, not bothering to try to prevent her head and knees from knocking against the walls of the small passageway.

Once on deck he stood her on her feet, held her tight against him, her back to his front, so she could see the ocean. She struggled, but silently, then suddenly twisted, trying to knee him in the balls with the side of her body. He held an arm tight around her neck until they were locked together tight. They were both breathing hard.

From across the deck Joe watched.

"Beg me," he said to her.

Her voice was nothing but defiance. "What you're doing is wrong."

Phantom picked her up, hefted her above his head in one motion.

"Beg me or you're going in," he said over the warm wind.

"Rot in hell, you bastard," she shouted back.

"You were right, Celeste: I have no morals. Very right."

He hurled her into the ocean. She slammed into the water, jackknifing like a fish to stay afloat. He watched her thrash expertly as the boat went by, estimated that she could survive a half hour if she kept it up.

Then she'd drown.

He turned away, shaking.

"Hey!" Joe came over, looking out at the swirling water around Celeste. "What's this about?"

"Just getting rid of the garbage."

"Shit. First you insist on taking her, and now you dump her? Fine, but let's do it right this time." He pulled out a gun, aimed it at the woman in the water. Phantom pushed his hand aside.

"No. She wanted to drown. I'm giving her her wish."

Joe lowered the gun, snorted, and shrugged. "You're the boss." They watched as the struggling woman got farther away.

Joe shook his head, grinned. "I thought you were sweet on her, the way you took care of her."

Phantom turned away, went below deck. He stood there a moment, then slammed his fist into the cabinet that housed the flotation vests. It made his fist hurt like hell, but it was a clean pain, not like what he felt inside. He did it again. Still, his throbbing fist didn't drown out what he was feeling in his stomach.

At least it wasn't the physical pain of impending death, which was what he'd left back at the Paradise hospital.

Another paradise awaited him now, he reminded himself. In another country, with palm trees and quiet beaches, where his money waited patiently for him. They would treat him right there, and for as long as he wanted. He had worked hard to buy himself another lifetime. He would get back what the angels had taken from him.

When they came, the tears surprised him.

"Shit, Celeste," he said to the air. He stood, stamped over to the radio, and phoned in to one of the islands.

"Man overboard," he told them, giving them the location

where he had thrown her in. "So get your asses out here and rescue her."

"Identify yourself."

"Fuck you," he said, disconnecting.

He yelled up a new course at Joe, one that would take them into the islands, where there were enough boats that they would be lost in the crowd and no one would link them with the injured woman in the ocean. By the time the rescue boat found Celeste and got her to talk, Phantom's boat would be through the islands and en route to their final destination.

And Celeste—if she managed to stay afloat for a half hour, and he was sure she could even in her injured state, they'd find her and she'd live.

He went above deck and looked out at the ocean, back toward where he'd left her. All he could see was blue ocean.

It should have pissed him off, to realize that she still had a piece of his heart, a piece he could not go back and claim without losing his life.

It didn't. He would live with what he had, and live without what he did not have. He would live without Celeste. He would live.

What really pissed him off was how the angels he had thought he had defeated were taking their share again.

ROMANCE, WITH MICE

I read the submission guidelines. They said:

"The Dadaoism Anthology will be the literary and psychic equivalent of a tour around the edges of a dying galaxy in a spectacularly malfunctioning space vehicle."

I couldn't resist the call. So I wrote this little romance that, yes, also has mice.

First published in *The Dadaoism Anthology*, Chomu Press, 2012.

THE STORY GOES LIKE THIS: Kate meets an older man. He's sensitive, insightful, and when he listens to her, she can feel it. They grow close quickly, very quickly, and within weeks she finds that she's falling for him.

He keeps her at arms length, never quite letting her in the door of his heart, despite the clear connection they have that blazes like a meteorite across both their skies.

She learns a lot about Marcus as they talk, daily, both from the things he says and the things he doesn't. But there's plenty about his past that he won't reveal.

Is he vulnerable? He is, but it's that kind of vulnerability that never goes all the way inside, that's close enough that you can hear it breathing, but stands just outside the door and won't come in.

They're sitting in the park here, today, side by side, not touching. They've barely touched in all these days that feel like years—a stroke across the fingers, a touch on the shoulder. Nothing more.

It's only been a few weeks, she tells herself.

She says, "you must know how I feel about you."

He nods slowly, not meeting her eyes, but they might as well be naked in each other's arms, the way it feels.

"So—" she says, haltingly. "I love you. You know that, right?"

He nods again.

Her words tumble out. "I want to know how you feel. It's okay if you don't love me back. What I mean to say is—"

"Stop," he says gently. "Don't do that. You know it isn't that. Love is—a word, just a word, but what's between us—" He turns to face her, meets her gaze, and his big blues capture her so thoroughly it's hard to remember anything else.

"Yes," he continues. "I love you and all that. And more. But."

"But what? Tell me." She's surprised at the force of her own words.

He looks away. He takes her hand, he puts it on his knee and strokes her fingers. Lines of fire, burning up her arms and into her heart and stomach and groin.

READER, let me ask you: do you feel it? The pull into the story? The way it's shaping up? Is it lovely? Agonizing? I hope you want me out of the way so you can get on with it.

Give me a moment.

I wrote this other story about a guy who paints. He's not right in the head, but he's not half bad with the art stuff, so he's sold some of his odd paintings for good money. That encouraged him to quit his day job, think of himself as an artist, and go through life looking at things slightly askew, as artists sometimes do.

The problem with thinking of yourself as a something is that you can get stuck there. Do you think of yourself as a reader? Is this story my story or is it, rather, yours?

This artist fellow, he paints with mice.

I know that sounds gross, but it's not. Or rather, I don't think it is. The truth is, I wasn't sure if he was using the mice to inspire his painting or somehow using their bodily fluids to make color. That was me being afraid to step into the story. I was younger then, and that's my only excuse.

I'm older now, mature and stuff, and I'm willing to go there with you, step into that story, find out, no holding back.

You with me?

Okay, let's go.

Here we are in his room, watching him paint. He pauses, takes a mouse from a cage. Ahha, look: he's not using the mouse to paint with, literally, as we might have feared. He doesn't take the little black-and-white creature in hand and smear it across the canvas. He doesn't bleed it to season his paints.

None of that. Rather, he holds each mouse gently, cupped between his hands, feels it quiver (that's what mice do when they're not eating, pooping, or fucking: they tremble), lets that fear come into him, take him over, make him vulnerable and open.

It is only then, when he has stripped away his protections, that the world seems immediate, vivid, alive. Only then can he let the art take him where it will. Color and shape make sense to him. He can see.

So why does he keep running out of mice, you wonder?

They escape into the walls, is why. Passion takes him over and he puts the creature down and starts in with his paints and the canvas. The mouse flees into the walls. (That's the other thing they do, mice, when they have a chance: flee into walls.)

And it's gone. That's why he runs out of mice.

In that moment when he holds this trembling life in his hands, he opens himself to the most intense experience he can. Only then can he hear the music of the universe and feel it flow through his paintbrush.

There. That story is finished. Thank you for joining me. Back to the other.

KATE IS SITTING on the park bench, thinking about Marcus and what he hasn't told her yet. The last time they sat on this bench together he said yes, next time I will tell you what the hell is going on here.

Since then, she's been twitching like a mouse cupped

inside her hunger for this strange man, wondering what the going-on could possibly be.

PTSD? She considers how he talks about the world, startles a little at loud noises. A vet who saw action?

Or something darker?

But he's been sweet and kind. Open in so many ways, except the ones that she wants most, the place she craves to go with him.

Which is, of course, not just physical. Meta-physical. It's the most amazing love she's ever felt. She doesn't care how old he is, or what he's got that he doesn't want to tell her about.

Whatever it is, illness or insanity, it doesn't matter. Amazing and epic love is worth a lot. She wants to go all the way with him. If there's a cost, she wants to know what it is. She can handle knowing.

He will tell her, she decides. He has to.

Across from the park is a vintage streetlamp clock. It's wrong. Still wrong, after all these years. Her phone's right, and he's due in minutes.

Kate takes a breath and rehearses what she's going to say. That she's an adult, she's got a right to know, that given what's between them, he needs to tell her. Whatever the cost, she's the one to decide if she'll pay it, not him.

"Here's the thing," he says, as he sits at her side. It's the first thing he says, not even hello. "You don't know what I know, and once you do, things can't be the same between us." He spears her with his gaze, blue eyes freezing a crack through her heart that opens to somewhere beyond lust.

"Hi," she exhales.

"Once I tell you, it's over between us. If I don't tell you, then, well, at least we have this." He gestures and she knows what he means.

He smiles, and it's a young smile, vulnerable, and oh so

sweet. She wants to kiss him more than she can remember ever wanting anything.

HEY, reader. Can you almost smell the end of this story? Do you feel it coming, how it might end?

How do you want it go?

"NO," she says. "I don't want to lose you. I love you."

"I know."

"You're saying that I can't have you."

He nods, but then shakes his head. "You can, but not the way you want."

"That's fucked up. I don't know what you could tell me that would change—" She trails off. She can, pretty quickly, come up with horrible things he could say. She feels sick.

He's look at her now, with that look that she can feel.

"Oh God," she says. She's trembling. He takes her hand and exhales slowly.

"Kate," he says. "I didn't realize it would go this way. I thought I was doing us both a favor. I thought—" he looks at the trees, the sky, at her. "I thought I could make things right. I didn't expect to fall for you, though I don't know how I could have been so incredibly stupid."

"Just tell me," she says. "Just—"

"I can't stay."

"What?"

"I kept meaning to tell you that I can't stay, but—" he gestures again, taking in the world around them, the world between them. "I didn't want to. I don't belong here. I just meant to talk to you a bit and go and—"

She doesn't understand what he's not saying, but she's suddenly certain that this is the inflection point, the moment after which it's all gone.

No, she decides. She grabs his shoulders and kisses him with all the hunger she's been holding and holding these weeks. It's like all the lights in the world turning on and turning off and turning on again. It's everything a kiss should be, could be, might be, ever was. It's the essence of kiss. It's fucking magic.

It goes on for a while as they both do this thing they have loudly and passionately not been doing these last three weeks.

When at last they come up for air, he has a stunned, scared look about him.

"Oh, God," he says.

"Yeah," she says, grinning.

He stands, steps back. It's a physical rejection, and hits her like a blow. He has the posture of a frightened animal. A mouse ready to dart.

"You're not mine," he says, angrily, his voice breaking. "I wish you were, you have no idea, but you're not."

She stands, too. "You can't decide that," she starts, but goes silent as he holds up a hand and blinks back tears.

"Give me a moment, my love. Hear me. Then I'll go."

"No." But she's not sure what she's saying no to.

"Listen: there's a man. He's got some real problems. But he's a good man, worth the trouble. At least I hope so. God, maybe he's not, but I swore to him that I'd come and plead his case to you. I ask you, I beg you, by everything that's passed between us, for the sake of this thing between us, give him a chance. And when he's exhausted that chance, give him another."

"No."

"Just remember what I've said. And Kate, I'm sorry."

"Marcus—"

He turns and runs, flat-out sprinting. She's so stunned, it takes her a moment to realize that he's leaving, that he'll be gone forever if she lets him.

She takes off after him. For a guy decades older he's surprisingly fast. He ducks into an alleyway. By the time she gets there—

You know. You do. He's gone.

Gone back to some future where he had managed to steal a time machine to come back to talk to the girl that he'd lost so many years ago, when he was young and immature and thought that being strong meant having opinions and not taking crap from anyone who could get under his skin.

He's gone. She'll search for him, of course. She'll come back to the park every day at all the times. She'll read "I saw U" posts. She'll answer her phone breathlessly. She'll sob into her pillow, night after night. She'll wonder if it was all a dream.

Then, one day, a year and change later, she'll see a guy on the street. Painfully familiar. Clean-shaven, where Marcus had a beard.

Could be Marcus's son. A younger brother.

It's not.

She'll throw good sense out the window and follow him around. She'll stop him right there on the street and stumblingly ask him out to coffee, and one thing will lead to another and—

AND IT WON'T BE the epic love affair it was with Marcus. He's a jerk in a lot of ways, immature and selfish. He doesn't know how to listen or open up. He's never held a mouse quivering in his hands. He doesn't even know about mice.

But she'll keep thinking of Marcus and what he said, and she'll keep giving this guy another chance.

Until one day when she realizes that he's not Marcus, and he isn't going to be, not for a long, long time.

She is not, she realizes, willing to wait decades for him to grow up. That price is too high.

STILL WITH ME, reader? Is this the ending you expected?

Me, neither.

But we're not quite done.

KATE HEALS WITH PAINT. She is not, when she puts brush to canvass, filled with passion. She does not hear the music of the universe, or feel anything flow through her paintbrush.

But there is healing in the spread of color across canvass, balm in the making of shapes.

On good days, she sees the world through a lens of creation.

On bad days, it's all the colors mixed together, a joyless sludge.

She keeps painting. She becomes more and more herself, tempered by the memory of her difficult time with Marcus the younger, and the stranger time with Marcus the older.

Into each of her love affairs, she takes a vision of how bright it could be. From each, she learns more about the beauty of trembling and the richness of sludge.

Years pass. Decades. Kate is nothing like her former self, and yet more like her than ever.

One day she'll run into Marcus again.

It's not the same park. It's not even the same city. But somehow, there they are, on a bench, together.

She'll stare at him, feeling chills and a lot of other things besides.

She'll say, "you owe me a hell of an apology."

He'll nod. "Without a doubt. But haven't I wasted enough of your time already?"

She will ponder this. Was it a waste? It is not so clear to her anymore, what is sludge and what is art.

"I'm sorry," he'll say. "Never again."

In that moment, Kate will realize that she's paid the costs, all of them. She'll look around and find the world bright and full of color.

A laugh will come to her. She'll take his hand.

They'll go for coffee.

Now we're done.

THE ANIMAL GAME

In 1993, anthology *Infinite Loop* called for science fiction stories by folks working in technology. I was an engineer and an author, knowledgeable and passionate about the promise of virtual reality.

VR games didn't exist yet. So in this story, I wrote one.

I didn't know this story was humor until I read it aloud and people started laughing. I caught on quickly, pausing to let the audience laugh in all the right places, hoping my surprise didn't show.

Yet another demonstration of how the author is often the last to know what they've created.

First published in Infinite Loop: *Stories About the Future by the People Creating It : Software Development's Own Anthology of Science Fiction*, Ed Larry Constantine, pub. Miller Freeman, 1993-

JAGUAR

ALAN LOVED A GOOD PUZZLE, even when it cost him by the hour. The Zoo cost, but it was worth it.

Last week Alan reached Level Three. He had no idea how, of course. Only the game masters knew how the Zoo's point system worked, or what "enhanced capabilities" you'd get on the next level, but they weren't talking. It was all very mysterious.

Alan loved it.

He'd been just a kid when he'd figured out that computer games were only as good as their designers. The challenge was to beat the game designer.

Now single-player games were too easy for him. Multiplayer games were where the challenge was, because even the best computers weren't as unpredictable and devious as the average person. Alan spent months in Dragon Defeat and Ultra-Civ before he got bored.

Then he bounced around from one multiplayer game to the next, looking for something different, something that demanded quick reflexes, fast thinking, and sound strategies, all at once. A game with plenty of puzzles to unravel.

Today he entered the Zoo early. Helmet on, strap down, and link in.

The Zoo book floated in front of him. Alan reached out gloved hands to open the book and browse tonight's games.

There was a separate game on each page, listing the number of players and a starting time. This time there was something new: a list of the other animals playing. Ah, his new Level Three capability. It was a small advantage, but every little bit helped. Now Alan could choose for his animal the one that would best suit the team, and the team made the game.

Whatever animals were on the team, the Zoo promised that the team could solve the game problem. But they didn't promise that your animal would be necessary. If you weren't needed, you had a walk-on part. It was always better to have a starring role.

Alan grabbed the fifth and last slot of game twenty-six, closing the game and starting the countdown clock. The team had a reasonable assortment of animals already, except for someone who was playing a baby iguana.

Probably a new guy. Oh well. Everyone had to learn some time.

BEAR

Joseph was in the Zoo practice room when the game closed and the countdown clock started ticking. He checked the Zoo book. A jaguar had bumped the game count to five.

He was still the only bear. Good. He'd been at Level Three for a while, and he wanted four so bad he could taste it. That's why he read the net discussions, for all the good it did.

What happened at higher levels? No one knew, but everyone had a theory. Mythical animals, someone said. Teams that survived across games. Dancing tomato plants. Then someone would claim to know for certain, and the flame wars would start again.

Joseph was certain that all the net discussions consisted of lies posted by other players to give themselves a competitive edge. So he fabricated a few himself, just to add to the general confusion.

The Zoo chair looked enough like a dental chair that Joseph had first had serious reservations. The Zoo cyberspace used more hardware than any other cspace game he'd seen. Cspace might be safer than driving a car, but Joseph wasn't going to risk his neck on the say-so of a statistician. He wanted to know what everything did, how it worked, and what the stop words were.

Now it was all familiar; an aide helped him strap down into the chair, and put on the helmet that provided the sight, sound, and smells that would make him experience the world as an animal would. Then the aide covered him with a wired blanket for temperature control, to let him feel the cold of a snow-covered land, or the sun on his fur. Realism, after all, was the thing.

He had been practicing as the Kodiak. There was the bear's strength, speed, and a great nose to compensate for lousy eyesight. The practice room was a personalized obstacle course that helped players figure out how their movements mapped onto the movements of their animals.

But the countdown had started, so he had a ten minute window to get into the game room. After that, the game was locked. He stepped out of the cspace practice room, and into the dressing room, which led to the game door.

The dressing room was covered with mirrors. Joseph admired himself: a massive, powerful, brown Kodiak bear. He held his paws in front of his face, flexed inch-long claws, and grinned.

The first time he'd won, he'd been a Kodiak bear. He'd been playing it ever since. You got used to your animal, its particular advantages, and so on. Besides, he'd kicked ass in that game, rescuing the princess from the tower with only seconds to spare. That was a rush, like nothing he'd ever known. When the rain of victory roses landed on them, he knew he was hooked.

Joseph looked up at the clock. It was time to kick ass again.

FALCON

Susanne had the best father in the world. He had gotten her out of school early again today, just to take her to her Zoo game. Dad said the Zoo was the best game anywhere for teaching problem solving. And he was an education game designer so he should know.

Her teachers didn't like it when she left early, but her grades were good and her father insisted, so she got to go. Her father said that as far as he was concerned, the Zoo games were more important than her classes. She knew it wasn't nice to tease, but she liked to tell her teachers what her father had said, especially when they got all stuck up about school being *so* important.

Today her father's meeting ran late and they almost missed Susanne's scheduled game. That would have been nasty—if you didn't show on time, you didn't get into the game.

Her dad set up his portable in the Zoo's waiting room and wished her a good game. One of the aides took her to a game room and helped her into the game chair.

She adjusted the helmet and mike. It was great: any sound she made into the mike, except the stop words sequence, would come out as the kinds of noises her falcon would make. Of course, you had to practice if you didn't want to sound like a sick turkey every time you talked. So she had practiced.

She'd tried lots of animals at first, but birds were the best, and the falcon was the best bird. Falcon was fast and could make really tight turns in mid-air. She didn't even think about the wheelchair when she was the falcon.

"Okay, let's go," she said to the mic. The room around

her faded and she was in the Zoo's mirrored dressing room. She was late; the countdown clock showed a minute to get through the game door.

Her reflection still looked like a boring girl mannequin. A menu floated down in front of her and she touched the picture of her falcon. The picture got brighter and larger.

There was a flash and the room was suddenly much larger. In the mirror she saw herself: dark eyes, gray head and back, and a cream-colored chest. She admired her wickedly sharp claws and grinned. The falcon in the mirror opened its mouth.

Flexing her shoulder muscles just so extended her wings. Another flex and the wings flapped. She took a deep breath and let out a loud cry, as loud as she could. The falcon's call seemed to come from her own chest, but it sounded like a falcon, not a girl.

The sound thrilled her, and made her heart beat faster. She did this every time. It put her into the right spirit for the game.

Twenty seconds left on the clock. She kicked and flapped aloft, hearing the familiar sound of her wings slicing through air.

Someone on the net had once told her that you could fly through the game door if you were a bird. Just fly through and it would open. She had been afraid to try at first, afraid it might not be true, afraid it might embarrass her.

Funny, the things that people let scare them. She pushed hard at the air, thrusting it all behind her. She shot toward the door. The door dissolved in front of her. She saw green.

ELEPHANT

Kelly had been in the practice room for hours. Every little movement did a lot when you were an elephant, so it was important to practice. She had been an elephant once before, and she had made a few mistakes.

Like stepping on a fellow player. She kept telling herself that they would have lost the game even without the badger, but she still remembered the crunching sound under her feet. This was the first time she had tried the elephant since then, and she had resolved to do better.

Besides, the elephant was harder than other animals. The trunk mapped onto her hand, and the Zoo chair gently prodded her feet so that she could tell when something was underneath her. After a few hours in the practice room she was sure she would notice if she stepped on a penny.

Or a badger. She entered the game room from the tiny dressing room. She took a big sniff and smelled only freshly cut grass, so she must be the first one to arrive.

She walked around the circular green clearing, flattening grass with each step. She looked behind her, to make sure it was only grass.

The Zoo did pretty well with mapping human senses onto animal ones, but there were always compromises. Animals that would be natural enemies in the wild were partners in the Zoo. Not only that, but your animal never got hungry and was never color blind. Kelly suspected the latter was pretty unrealistic, but the Zoo was a business, after all, and market pressures demanded that the game be more fun than it was realistic.

And it was fun, even though Kelly wasn't much of a gamer. Most computer games were a mindless waste of time. More sophisticated technology just meant that flight simulators and zap 'em up games had more visual realism, but it was still the same old stuff. What was the point of playing against a computer? The computer always won, unless it let you win. But in the Zoo you played with other people. Real people. That was how you won, by working as a team.

And to be an elephant, like she was now; to step heavy and still have sensitive feet. It was the closest you could get to reincarnation in one life.

At the center of the clearing was a white marble pedestal. There was a small, golden plaque mounted near the top. Kelly had already read the plaque twice. It said:

"The Milnak bauble is a cherished heirloom of the gnomish dancers, who come every spring to contemplate the meaning of the bauble's flawless, mirrored perfection."

There was a small, sphere-shaped depression on the top of the pedestal. It was empty.

IGUANA

David was perfectly happy to admit that he had been wrong.

When he had left the Zoo project some four years ago, the software had been a mangled, spaghetti-like mess, and the bank wouldn't give them the loan they needed for expensive cspace equipment. The others had hand-waved his warnings away, and pushed blithely on. David had seen the writing on the wall, and he didn't want to be there when it all came crashing down.

He might have stayed if not for the kids and the mortgage. The Zoo looked risky then, and he couldn't afford the risk.

But he wasn't happy about it. He'd designed a big chunk

of the Zoo's software and put in a lot of time and sweat. He wanted the Zoo to succeed.

And it finally had. After he left.

So he'd been more than a little surprised to hear from his old Zoo cronies last month. They wanted to know, since the Zoo had been in the black for nearly a year, would he like to come back?

If they were willing to forget that he had left when the chips were down, maybe he could forget that they ignored his warnings. He wanted to think it over, take a look at what they'd done with the Zoo, and see if it was worth his time.

Sure, they said, handing him unlimited game access. Take your time. But decide by the end of next week, and now that was tomorrow.

He'd played a lot in the last two weeks, to try to see the game from the user's perspective. He wanted to know what they'd done to his work, but of course they wouldn't show him any code until he came on board. So he poked around, looked for boundary conditions, and generally tried to crash the program.

But he still wasn't sure. Maybe his career should move beyond games.

Maybe he'd play one more game before he decided. He nosed open the large game room door and wriggled in. Another countdown clock appeared unobtrusively in the upper left corner of his field of vision. This game was an hour long.

High, green stalks surrounded him. Grass, he realized, feeling a little dumb. He looked over his shoulder. The door had vanished. If he lifted his head, he could sort of see the top halves of three mountains that were shaped roughly like animals: a bear, a big cat, and an elephant. He could feel them move, by the vibration and subsonics under his feet.

This baby iguana was the tiniest animal David had tried

yet. He was impressed at how effectively the Zoo cspace made him feel small. Between the jungle of grass and the vibrations, he was convinced that if he didn't do something quick, one of his teammates would step on him.

He yelled at them. His iguana mouth opened, and no sound came out. Right, he remembered belatedly, iguanas don't have vocal chords.

Time for something inventive. He twisted his body back and forth in the grass, moving the green stalks around him. A bird cried overhead, and he looked up. The bird looked big enough to swallow him in one gulp. He hoped it was on his team.

The ground shook again. The mountains circled him and their heads became much larger as they bent down for a closer look. He opened his mouth and tasted the animal smells around him.

The heads looked at each other and then back at him. He looked up at them. The stamp of human surprise on their animal faces made him laugh. A little hiss came from his mouth.

If they were wondering what he was good for, they weren't alone. The software he'd written for the Zoo tried to include every animal on the team in the game puzzle's solution. Sure, the Zoo would do fine with lions and tigers and bears, but what would it do with a baby iguana?

The elephant pointed at the nearby white marble pillar. David craned his neck, but he couldn't see the top of the pillar. He hoped it wasn't important.

The big cat made a sound, a throaty stutter, and pointed with a paw. He began to walk away with the bear and the elephant.

David was already regretting his animal choice. He couldn't see much and now he discovered that he couldn't keep up, either. He followed the vibrations of the elephant's footsteps, wriggling to catch up, but he just couldn't match the pace.

He could drop out of the game with stop words, but calling it quits would stop the game for everyone on the team. That was one of the rules, intended to keep everyone playing together. It worked.

Besides, he wanted to see what his program could do, now that it was all grown up.

JAGUAR

The goal was clear and simple: find the silver bauble and put it back on the pedestal.

The elephant and the bear followed him along the game path. The falcon circled above, screeching, over and over. It was starting to get on Alan's nerves. Alan never made noises for no reason. Noise was too useful to waste. It was a signal, a danger sign. Like a car horn. This was part of the game, he knew. Some players liked the sound of their own voices. You couldn't pick who you played with, so you had to live with it. Sooner or later the bird would get bored and stop. He hoped.

Unless, of course, Alan thought suddenly, the bird was signaling something. He looked back.

The iguana. Alan growled softly at himself for missing the obvious. He caught the elephant's eye and nodded toward where the iguana was. Last.

Someone would have to carry the stupid animal. He had no idea why someone would pick to play an iguana. It was slow, small, and in constant danger of getting crushed.

The elephant had turned back. It reached down and picked up the iguana with its trunk, then put the iguana on its forehead.

Back on the game path, Alan led, the bear and the elephant followed, and the falcon—now silent—tracked them from the air.

They came to a deep, fast-moving river that cut across the game path that they were obviously meant to follow. The bear pushed past Alan and waded into the water.

Alan shook his head at the bear's recklessness. Who knew what dangers might lurk in the river? Alan shrugged. Let the bear take the risks.

He and the elephant waited until the bear came up the other side, dripping wet. Alan jumped in, swam across, and pulled himself up on the other shore. He looked back to see the tip of the elephant's trunk above the water.

A convenient way to cross the river, with that built-in snorkel. But wait—where was the iguana?

Alan looked around frantically for the iguana as the elephant slowly rose out of the water.

No iguana. The elephant looked at Alan and its eyes went wide. It patted its forehead and headed back into the river, snaking its trunk across the water.

There it was—a small wriggle on the river, quickly heading downstream. Alan bounded along the grassy bank, dodging trees and brush. He had been in enough games to be sure that the river would shortly lead to a majestic, rock lined waterfall, perfect for smashing little reptiles into little bits.

The current picked up speed, and the iguana was wriggling around, vainly trying to swim. Alan caught up to the iguana, but now he'd have to dive in and try to pick the iguana out of the rushing water with his mouth. Without crushing it. That would be some trick.

Here they were, not three minutes into the game, about to lose a player. Alan had been through this before. Sometimes you could win without all the animals you'd started with, but not often.

He glanced ahead and picked a spot where he would launch himself into the river. Once there, he crouched, readied himself for the jump, and nearly tripped over his front paws as he tried to stop himself.

He'd seen it as he was about to jump, the falcon up high, diving down. The falcon hit the water and cut through with a splash, then was climbing again into the sky. Alan looked around, not sure if the falcon had managed to pick out the small iguana. He looked up, and there it was, a small green shape wiggling in the falcon's claws.

Alan trotted back along the bank. When he arrived, the falcon was standing on the elephant's head, the iguana next to him.

Impressive. Alan gave the bird a nod of respect. The elephant touched the iguana gently with its trunk-fingers, and made a sound through its trunk.

First disaster averted, Alan thought, and fifty minutes to go. He exhaled slowly.

BEAR

At least the bird had some sense. Maybe it had traded brains with the elephant. Sure, that was it. That would explain how the elephant could take a bath in the river with an iguana on its head. Talk about stupid.

The lizard was a lot of trouble. They might be better off losing him, but it was better to hedge your bets and keep all the players alive as long as possible. Joseph had learned that the hard way.

And besides, the daring rescue might earn them style points, if there was anyone watching the game. Style mattered; you could lose the game and still get style points.

Winning was tough enough. You had to take what you could get.

The jaguar was taking the lead again. Good. Self-appointed leaders usually got killed first. Leadership, insofar as there was a leader in a game where no one could talk, usually fell to the fastest animal in the bunch. The cat was pretty fast, though Joseph doubted the cat could take him and win. Too bad it wasn't that kind of game, so he couldn't find out.

Well, he could find out, but it would probably cost him the game. A win in this game could bump him up to Level Four. He could smell it in the air.

The road had begun to narrow as they walked up to the top of a hill. The banks on either side of the path sloped sharply up, forming a steep ravine. Trees grew at the top of the banks on either side, and stones littered the path. It was an odd transition for the land to make.

So odd, in fact, that Joseph started to get suspicious. That was why he saw the boulder first.

It materialized out of nowhere at the top of the hill. It rocked a little, then started slowly rolling down toward the group.

Joseph gave a loud warning growl. The jaguar was turning around, obviously trying to figure out what to do. The cat was too slow; Joseph was already in action. He waved the bird toward the elephant with his paw, hoping the bird would take the hint. It did; it swooped, grabbed the lizard, and flew up to the safety of a nearby tree.

Joseph could feel the ground shake as the boulder picked up speed. It was a steep climb out of the ravine, but he and the cat were both climbers. They bounded up opposite sides.

That took care of everyone. Except the elephant. The big beast tried to climb out of the ravine by running up the side and grabbing a bush. The bush pulled out of the ground and the elephant slid back down.

For a split second Joseph considered letting the boulder simply roll into the elephant. The team might do better without the big, blundering, brainless beast. There was a solution to saving the elephant, but it wasn't obvious. If he let the elephant die, no one could fault him.

On the other hand, saving the elephant might win him style points.

Joseph leaned on a nearby tree, bending it down toward the elephant, but not close enough to grab. He growled and patted the tree significantly. He half-hoped the elephant wouldn't take the hint, and would just stand there in the path of the boulder. He wondered what it would look like to see it crushed.

The timing was critical, because the tree wouldn't hold the elephant for long. When the boulder was close, he used his weight to put the tree just out of reach of the elephant.

The elephant made a scared, air-filled sound, scrambled up the slope, and grabbed the tree's trunk with its own. The elephant's momentum, coupled with its trunk-hold on the tree was enough to take it out of the path of the boulder long enough for the boulder to pass by.

Joseph scrambled away from the tree. The elephant let go, sliding noisily back down into the ravine. The tree snapped back.

Growling triumphantly, Joseph shook his paw at the receding boulder. That should earn him style points, if anything could.

ELEPHANT

Kelly's heart was still pounding from the close call with the boulder, but she felt good. Really good.

She touched the iguana on her forehead. Just to be sure. When they crossed the river, Kelly had been coming close to the deeper elephant self within. She had stopped thinking in words, as she concentrated on the sights and sounds around her. So fully immersed was she in the experience, that she had forgotten all about the iguana until she got out of the water.

If the bird hadn't saved the iguana, if an animal died because of her again—she couldn't take it. She would have left the game.

But it was the boulder that brought it all home. If the bear hadn't helped her, she would be out of the game now. The bear had smiled so encouragingly at her as it patted the tree, telling her in bear-talk how to grab hold and be safe from the boulder. The bear's final, protective growl at the boulder as it went by made her feel all warm inside.

The bear was willing to help her, even after she had nearly lost the iguana in the river. The bear had shown her that she had been selfish when she thought of quitting before. They were a team, the bear said in bear-talk, not just a group of players.

Now she understood. She wasn't just an elephant, she was part of something greater. A team. Bear, she decided, was very wise.

They topped the hill and started down the other side. There was something metallic in the meadow below, something that sparkled in the sun. As they got closer, Kelly saw that there was a metal door in the middle of the road.

The falcon sat on top of the door and Kelly walked around the other side. Curious. On one side it was a door, and on the other it was just a hard, door-sized black rectangle.

The metal side of the door had a small keyhole, just below a notched doorknob. She tried the knob, but the door was locked.

The bear growled and pushed her aside. Bear seemed gruff, but she knew better. Bear was really very kind and generous. And her friend. She moved aside as quickly as she could.

The bear threw himself against the door. The falcon took off with a cry and landed a distance away. The bear stepped back further and threw himself at the door again, and again, making the metal door ring with the impact, but not making it open.

The jaguar growled and waved a paw at the bear. Jaguar scratched at the door furiously, like a cat at a couch. But when he was done, there was no mark on the door.

Kelly snorted and waved the cat and bear aside. Why was it that all some animals could think of was how to use their brute force? Kelly shook her head. She felt around in the grass by the door, searching for a key.

The jaguar caught on, and started sniffing around the door. After a minute the cat chuffed and dug into the ground with its paws, scattering grass and dirt. The cat stepped back. Kelly felt in the hole and brought out a dirt-covered metal key.

Now she knew what her purpose in the game was. *Fingers.* She wiped the key on the grass to clean it off, and then inserted it in the door lock. She turned the key. The lock clicked.

This was the moment to savor, she decided. She wasn't just a part of the team, but an essential part. This was what the game was about. This was why she was meant to be an elephant.

Kelly turned the doorknob and pulled the door open. Inside was a torch-lit corridor.

Her elation and smile faded as the jaguar and bear darted around her into the doorway. The falcon grabbed the iguana off her head and flew in after them. They vanished around a corner at the end of the hallway.

Now she had to wait until they came back. She was just too big to get through the doorway.

***

FALCON

It wasn't hard to fly with the iguana in her claws, at least not for short distances, but it changed her lift and navigation, which was particularly annoying when she was trying to get through halls and doorways.

Well, she'd had enough. With a cry that echoed against the stone walls, she put the iguana down in front of the bear, who could carry the iguana as well as she could. The bear slowed, growled a bit, and then picked up the iguana, cupping the iguana in its paws as they walked.

Susanne shrugged her shoulders and ruffled her wings. Sunlight from the open door behind them followed them only to the first turn. Then their shadows flickered in torchlight against stone walls.

They came to another door: simple, wooden, and with no keyhole. The bear waved them out of the way, and threw himself heavily against the door, which flew right open. Susanne chuckled as the startled bear sailed into the room.

In the center of the room was a swimming pool, complete with diving board, blue tile, and depth markers, but no water. Instead the pool was completely filled with small, silver baubles.

The bear and the cat looked at each other and then back at the pool. The jaguar gave a short growl. The bear shook his head.

There had to be thousands of baubles in the pool. Could they use any one? Susanne didn't think so. Which one, then?

Thirty minutes to go. She kicked, flapped aloft, and glided over the pool, looking down on the array of silver balls. What was she looking for? There had to be a clue somewhere.

The cat sniffed at the baubles from the edge of the pool, then put a paw in. The paw began to sink and he pulled back.

Susanne flew back the other way, still looking. Something different, something special. One bauble out of thousands. The puzzle could be solved. She just had to keep trying.

On her fifth pass she saw a quick, colored gleam and gave a victory cry. The bauble was half-hidden under several other baubles. She dove with a precision she had practiced hard to get, grabbed the bauble and landed on the side of the pool. She put the bauble on the floor near the jaguar and bear, so that they could see the red "X" on it. They both nodded at her, so she picked up the bauble and flew out the door. Jaguar and bear followed.

Once outside, Susanne decided that she didn't want to bet the game on her ability to carry the bauble safely back, so she put the bauble down in front of the elephant, who picked it up and brought it close to one eye. The jaguar and elephant headed back along the game path. The bear put the iguana down near Susanne and followed.

She yelled a protest at the bear. Short distances were fine, but for this flight she'd be hundreds of feet up in the air; the iguana would be safer with the bear. She yelled again, but the other three animals were already far down the path and ignored her.

She looked at the iguana. She felt dismay, then sympathy. Poor little guy. She knew what it was like, being dependent on others just to get around. In the Zoo that wasn't a problem for her. Here she could forget the daily frustrations of life in a wheelchair, and enjoy the freedom of being a falcon.

But now the iguana was stuck. It was odd, being on the other side of things.

The iguana blinked at her. She stepped over it, carefully avoiding the delicate green ridges. Maybe she could carry it. She'd have to try.

Still she hesitated. What, she asked herself, was the worst thing that could possibly happen?

She could drop him, that's what.

But it was only a game. Right? Sometimes you won, sometimes you lost, and sometimes you died. But if you waited for things to fall into your lap, you'd wait a long time.

She took hold of the iguana, resolved not to let go, no matter what, and took to the air.

IGUANA

David admired the scenery the Zoo software had constructed. Here in the falcon's grip it was all he could do.

It was better than catching only glimpses of the action through the bear's claws. Oddly, he felt more secure in the falcon's claws; David half-expected the bear to crush him or drop him. And it had been no picnic, clinging to the elephant's head, hoping that the moving mountain would stay under him.

But he finally had a clue to the game puzzle. The baubles in the swimming pool, the falcon flying back and forth, grabbing the bauble marked with the red "X." The bauble was the game's win condition.

A win would be nice. In the two weeks he'd been playing, his team hadn't won once.

And that made him suspicious. Would the game masters tilt the odds in his favor to give him a win and maybe sway his decision to take the job? Sure, he'd like to see a winning game, but if it wasn't fairly won, well...

He smirked at his own internal struggle. Here he was, one of the original Zoo game masters, worrying about whether he would win the game fairly.

Sure, he decided, he'd take an easy win just to see what happened, but he would think of it as a demo. And while it was flattering to think of his old partners wanting him back enough to stack the deck in his favor, it just wasn't right.

The falcon dropped down from the sky and David's stomach flip-flopped. The bird left him in front of the bear again, who growled before picking him up.

They were all gathered around the pedestal. The elephant put the bauble on top and took a few steps back.

This was it. Win time. The bauble began to glow. It turned orange, then red, then white, and a high-pitched sound filled the air. There was a sudden, audible *crack* as the bauble fell apart into pieces. The pieces glowed and darkened, then crumbled into a red, pollen-fine dust that blew away in the breeze.

The animals exchanged wide-eyed looks. David felt disappointment mixed with relief. The win hadn't been easy, after all.

The wrong bauble. Too bad. Somewhere back in the swimming pool, he guessed, was the right bauble. The "X" had been a decoy. He wondered what else might distinguish one bauble from the rest.

And then he had it.

He started thrashing his tail against the bear's paw to get its attention.

Fifteen minutes left. Not enough time. It couldn't possibly be enough time.

FALCON

Susanne saw the iguana wriggling around in the bear's paw, which seemed like a good way to get dropped. Not that it mattered now; they'd lost the game.

They had fifteen minutes left. She might as well say her stop words and end the game instead of waiting for the clock to run out.

The iguana was still wriggling. Stupid lizard. Couldn't he see that he was just being difficult now that they'd lost? The game was over and—

Oh.

Maybe the iguana had an idea. She looked around. They were all just standing there, looking dazed. All but the iguana.

Well, if the iguana had something—what did they have to lose? They needed the right bauble, Susanne reasoned. There was only one place to get another bauble.

Susanne kicked off the elephant's head, from where she had watched the bauble break apart. She flapped aloft and dove, grabbing the iguana out of the bear's paw before the bear could react.

She was getting good at that particular move.

Below, the bear growled loudly at her, shaking his paw skyward. She chuckled. Not her fault that he was ground-locked. And not paying attention.

The land went by below, as she gripped the iguana,

tightly, but not too tightly. She flew as fast as she could, thinking of herself as a streamlined bullet of beak and feathers. And iguana.

ELEPHANT

Kelly thought frantically. She had put the bauble on the pedestal— that was right, wasn't it?—and the bauble had turned red and self-destructed. And then the bird grabbed the lizard and started flying back up the path.

What had she done wrong? And why were they going back?

The jaguar was motioning with his head, at Kelly and the bear, and then he took off at a dead run back up the path. Kelly and the bear followed.

She went over it one more time. She had put the bauble on the pedestal. And it had blown up. She must have done something wrong. She felt terrible. She thought she was doing so well. Had she missed something? Something a real elephant would have seen?

She'd made them lose, somehow. But if they'd already lost, why were they going back?

Could there be another bauble, somewhere inside the steel door? That had to be it; there was another bauble, the right bauble, and now they were going back to get it.

She snorted. That was silly; they should have brought both baubles out with them the first time. If she had been with them, she would have done it herself.

They swam across the river and loped up the incline. When they arrived at the door, the big cat and the bear ran in, leaving her behind again.

Next time she would be a horse. Or maybe a cheetah. Anything that would fit through that damned door.

And now they were down to ten minutes.

BEAR

Joseph had suspected it was too good to be true, finding the right bauble so early in the game, and it was.

Of course, he wasn't entirely without blame. "Mirrored perfection" was an obvious hint that didn't include a bauble with markings. He'd missed that.

He was still growling at the bird, who wisely stayed out of his way. He would rip the bird apart if he could get close enough. You gave a warning call before you flew close to another animal. It was pure stupidity to surprise someone on your side. Especially someone with claws.

He had picked up the iguana so that the lizard could see the bauble on top of the pedestal, an act of generosity toward a useless player. What did he get for it? A dive-bombing falcon in his face. Next time he wouldn't bother.

He watched the bird as it flew back and forth over the pool, its eyes on the iguana. The iguana was scampering across the pool of silver baubles. It was light enough not to sink down between the baubles. The iguana was so small that each bauble was nearly as large as its head.

This was absurd. They would do as well if they picked up as many of the baubles as they could carry, and took them back to the pedestal before the clock ran out. He could carry a few in his paws, and some in his mouth, if he remembered not to swallow.

He moved toward the edge of the pool. The jaguar growled at him and blocked his path. He growled back.

If the stupid cat didn't let him past, there was no question of them winning. And to hell with style points.

He took a swipe at the jaguar. The cat backed to the edge of the pool, its ears flat. It growled again and shook its head, a clear message that the jaguar didn't want to fight.

Joseph didn't care. He took another step forward.

IGUANA

There was just no way David could touch all the baubles. Even if the pool was only a foot deep, he would still miss most of them. There were just too many.

But this was clearly the trick, this was what the iguana was supposed to do, so it should be possible, even if it was unlikely.

The metallic balls shifted a little under him as he walked across. He tried to touch as many as he could. It had to be here somewhere.

Then he found it. He felt the heat against his stomach, a sharp contrast to the coolness of all the other metal balls he had touched.

Iguanas were good at identifying subtle temperature differences. As cold-blooded animals, they had to be.

He heard the jaguar growl somewhere behind him and an answering snarl from the bear.

He nosed the ball he had identified, hoping the falcon was watching, hoping it would understand.

FALCON

Susanne couldn't believe it. Here they were, with only seven minutes to win the game, and the cat and the bear were squaring off with each other.

They were worse than schoolyard brats. If they wanted that kind of game, there were plenty around. They shouldn't screw up everyone else's game at the same time.

She inhaled deeply, and let out the loudest, most piercing cry she could. The bear and the cat looked up at her, their spat momentarily interrupted.

The iguana touched its nose against one of the silver balls. Then it did it again.

That was it, then. She didn't know how he knew, but it was their last, best chance.

She dove for the ball, grabbed it in her claws without touching the iguana, and flew out through the hallway and the steel door. She dropped the bauble on the ground by the elephant, flew back in, and retrieved the iguana from the pool. The cat and the bear followed behind, their fight apparently less interesting than the possibility that they might win with this bauble.

This time there was no question of her flying back with the iguana. No one else could make it in time. She dropped the iguana, picked up the bauble, and took to the skies. The ground-locked animals were running full speed along the game path below her. She gave it all she had, concentrating with every wing stroke, looking forward to the clearing, the pedestal, and a possible victory.

She just hoped there was enough time.

JAGUAR

As Alan came into the clearing, the game clock ticked to all zeros. He had passed the bear and the elephant some time ago. He hoped one of them had remembered to bring the iguana.

The falcon sat on the edge of the pedestal, staring at the silver ball.

The bauble glowed white, like a light bulb. The sound of chimes, or bells, filled the air around them.

It was a sound Alan knew. He had heard it only a few times before. Alan threw his head back and gave his victory whoop, which came out as a loud roar. The falcon must have been startled—it took to the air and scolded him.

The bear and elephant arrived, the iguana securely wrapped in the elephant's coiled trunk. The five of them gathered around the pedestal.

Alan had some idea of what would happen next, but it varied from game to game. The first time he had won, roses and stars had fallen down on the animals from the sky, while dozens of small monkeys danced around them to the sound of triumphant horns. When the ground was covered with roses, the game landscape had faded and Alan had found himself back in his dressing room. The next time Alan won, a single monkey came out and gave them each a wreath of violet roses.

Alan wondered if the dancing monkeys were constructs or game masters. A single monkey walked out of the trees toward them. It held a dozen purple roses in one arm.

The monkey stopped in front of the elephant, who had put the lizard down nearby. The monkey held out a rose to the elephant, who waved its trunk and then took the flower delicately in its trunk-fingers.

"Good job," the monkey said to the elephant.

Alan blinked, stunned. Spoken words? In the Zoo? After scores of games, Alan had stopped even hoping.

But if they could *talk* to each other—

The elephant made a short sound, like the clearing of a water-logged trumpet. Then the elephant slowly faded. Alan saw the rest of the clearing through the elephant before the creature vanished completely.

The monkey walked to the bear and held out another rose.

"Nice work," the monkey said.

The bear gave a loud growl, shook its paws above its head, and took the rose between two large paws. The bear faded and disappeared.

The monkey went to the falcon and offered it a rose. The falcon took the flower in its beak.

"Impressive," the monkey said to the bird. Alan nodded his agreement.

And then there was only Alan and the iguana.

"Carry on," the monkey said to Alan, with a smile and a rose. Alan nodded, and bent his head to take the offered rose between his teeth.

As the clearing began to fade around him, Alan saw the monkey offering the remaining eight roses to the iguana, who was nodding, as if in answer to a silent question.

All those roses, just for the iguana? But why?

Another puzzle.

Alan chuckled.

SHELTER FROM THE STORM

A story and its author are intimately connected. We affect each other. As creators, we enter into the story and world we're creating. Eventually, we come back.

Sometimes it's delightful. Sometimes unnerving.

Sometimes, it's darker.

To write Susan Langley I had to become her for a time. To think as she did, to see the world as she did.

I wasn't the same after that. I couldn't be. I'd taken a journey into a very different mind, and there was no way I could come back to myself unchanged.

I've written more than a few stories about the edges of sanity. But that's not safe work: to find the edges of anything, you have to cross the line.

I sometimes wonder if walking this landscape and becoming comfortable with the cliff edges is what's kept me sane. Something like sane. Differently-sane, perhaps.

First published in *Leather Tomes and Spiderwebs*, edited by Blaze Ward and Leah Cutter, 2018.

GRAMMA UNDERSTOOD. When the nights were dark beyond bearing, I'd climb the stairs to her room, forcing myself to forget each stair as I passed. She snored a bit as I sat on her thick featherbed. Then she woke and took my hand.

"The darkness will fade, Susie. Really it will. You'll see."

And it did. But the light, when it came, was not much better. It made the walls weep and the doors scream until all I wanted to do was join them.

But I knew better. I was silent when the judge gave my brother a long, hard look. The light came through the high windows of the courtroom and shattered across the room like glass, raining down on all our bare heads.

"You ought to be ashamed, Mr. Langley. Motion denied." He turned his judge's attention on me. "Ms. Langley, my most sincere condolences on the loss of your grandmother."

I nodded and looked down at my feet, seeing their shoes, proper shoes, remembering the battle I had this morning getting my toes into them.

"Thank you, your honor," I said softly.

WHEN I REMEMBERED, I'd pull on my robe, take the basket of nails, and go down the stairs to the basement where I kept her. I would pull the sheet off, let it slide to the floor, and hold my breath for a moment. Just in case.

She stared vacantly and never at me. It bothered me that she didn't look at me but I resolved not to take it personally. Considering what I did to her, I figured we were about even.

The nails only went in about a quarter inch but that was all I needed. I spelled my name across her chest years ago, but that seemed so childish that I had pulled them all out and filled in the holes. Now I was hammering in a garter belt for her, complete with lace frill, made of shiny silver nails.

Finishing nails, they call them. As if I would ever be done. But still.

It wasn't for lack of anything better to do that I found my way down there, nor was the day so hot and sunny that the idea of looking out the window made my skin craw as it so often did in the long days of summer; rather I felt an obligation to dress her in the regalia that best suited her plastic skin and steel bones. She deserved the best.

I named her every week. I got new names from the noise-box, as I went about my work, dusting the piano that I never used, and cutting potatoes into small animal shapes. I hid from the mailman because I knew he regarded me with pity and thought me mentally deficient, and I wanted to let the mail sit a while after his touch so that it would not contaminate me with his small-minded sympathies.

The cat at the window I never touched. He didn't like it, though he accepted the food and water I set out on the ledge for him when it occurred to me to do so. He left me small, broken animals, mice and birds, lying limp on my window sill. It seemed a good trade.

In the evenings she walked the basement as I lay in bed. The nails that clothed her and made up her boots and bra clicked together as she went through her cheerleading exercises.

She chanted victory for the Foxes, her high school team. I had gone to a rival school so I lay still for fear she would hear me breathing and come upstairs. I knew from clothing her how strong she was. I shivered in bed at night, despite the locks on the basement door, terrified what she would do if she ever discovered me here. I listened for hours to her until finally in the very early morning she would quiet and I could sleep.

Mornings were gentle in fall and winter, but summer mornings were loud. I would calm them with the pills, and the morning would go back to sleep until afternoon. Afternoons were busy times, times of cleaning, of checking the piano for spiders and the carpet for fallen objects that would become lost forever if I did not find them first.

THE DOORS inside my house are not really doors. They are pieces of wall that move. They obey me when I open or close them, though I can't say why. Sometimes I hear them whispering about destiny and choice and rebellion. They have not yet refused to let me through, but I suspect the day may come. I tell them they are the finest doors that money can buy, hoping my flattery will inspire their cooperation. But they are not really doors.

A real door is one that goes outside. It does not whisper or consider its destiny, though sometimes it weeps. It exists to cause change, to break down the card towers that I build, and to let in the animals who want to bite me and make the carpet wet with my blood. The door is not my friend, but it is my door, and so I have an obligation.

That's the door through which they come. Victor, with his papers and black metal pen and childish words. He thinks I'm simple, and he's always surprised when I sign the right papers and eat the ones that would give him too much candy. He's stupid and weak but the door lets him in anyway. Because it's a real door.

I WAS in the bathroom making water sculptures when the door screamed. I screamed back and screamed again to show it I wouldn't be bested. Then I hid.

Screaming is usually enough to make the door stop but

this time it just kept going and I couldn't bear it so I got out of the tub and ran to it. I fell to my knees and begged it to stop, to go back to sleep.

Suddenly the door was quiet. I looked up.

A dark figure stood on the other side of the twisted glass. I understood now why the door reacted that way. I lay down on the floor and watched the dark figure from the unambiguous perspective of the floor.

The figure hit the glass. That was rude. I growled up at it. Again: hit and hit.

There was no other way, so I got up, and put my face against the cold glass.

"Stop it!" I shouted.

It hit the glass again.

I don't like the door and the things it lets in but it's my door and I have to live with it. The last time someone hit the door this hard it whimpered all night long. I had to turn on the noise box as loud as it would go.

I grabbed the door, twisted and pulled. I ached for the poor thing but I was out of options.

The man stared at me. He opened his mouth.

"Go away," I yelled, hoping to keep him from talking.

"Ms. Langley?"

I remembered what Gramma said before she left for the last time: "Try to be polite, sweetness."

Okay, Gramma.

"Eat shit and die," I said, very politely. "And stop hitting my door."

"I'm your new doctor. May I come in?"

The door held its breath and shut its eyes. We both wanted this over. I patted it and made what I hoped to be reassuring cooing sounds but were mostly a sort of gargle.

My doctor, Marlow, had grey hair and talked slowly. This man was young, with dark hair and dark eyes.

"I don't need a new doctor. The old one works just fine."

"Ah," he said, drawing it out, "I'm afraid that's not quite true. Dr. Marlow has suffered a stroke. He's not well. You've been assigned to me."

"I don't want you."

He laughed and shook his head.

I bared my teeth and growled.

"Please," he said, gesturing at me.

"What do you mean, 'please'?"

"You're naked," he said, as if that explained everything. One of his hands kind of flipped up, as if begging for candy. "If someone comes by, this might look a little—odd. May I come in?"

I shook my head and laughed. It was funny, just how stupid they thought I was.

"Let's see some ID," I said, trying to sound nasty. "And your letter of introduction."

He produced a wallet, the brown kind. He opened it and pulled out a card with his picture on it, held it out for me to see. I took the card and the wallet, too. I went through it all, piece by piece. He began to fidget.

"You're lucky I know how to read," I told him.

"Yes," he said, "I am."

"Well," I said after I'd looked it all over, "all this looks like the plausible possessions of a doctor. Only forty seven dollars?" I smirked. "Let me see your credit cards."

He reached into a coat pocket and pulled out a small plastic folder with brightly colored cards in it. I checked the signature against the ones in his wallet, and counted the different colors.

"Five," I told him. "Very doctor-like. Show me the letter."

"Give me back my wallet and credit cards first."

I tried not to laugh, and failed, giggling as I handed the mess back to him.

He pulled an envelope from inside his jacket, just like they do on the noise-box, and handed it to me. I held the envelope at arm's length, opened it slightly, and peered inside. Got to be careful. I pulled it out.

"Look," I whispered, awestruck, showing it to the door, unfolding it slowly. "See how carefully it's been creased? I mean, God, it's perfect. So we know he didn't do it. Do you think his secretary spent hours getting the fold just right?"

He started to speak and I cut him off. "Not asking you," I said. "Be quiet."

At the bottom of the letter was a signature. I know signatures. It was Marlow's.

Ah hell.

I cuffed the door. It whimpered.

I read the letter. Marlow was deserting me, the bastard. I needed him. I paid him, and he was deserting me. This guy was taking over.

"All right," I said. "So what do you want?"

"To come in," he said.

"Why?"

"Because," he said, in that doctor tone of voice, the one where they seem to be struggling to explain the obvious to you, as a personal favor, "your file says you never leave your house, so I can't see you in my office. You don't have a phone, so I can't call you. As your doctor, I have to see you before I can prescribe drugs for you. Now, I don't usually make house calls—"

"That's so very nice. What do you want, brownie points?"

"No," he said. "I want to come in."

I thought about it. It was still mid-day, so she probably wouldn't hear us, not with all the light crashing around.

"All right," I said, "but don't touch the door."

He picked up his doctor-bag, and I stood aside to let him pass. As instructed he didn't touch the door. I gave him some respect, but it was grudging. As I closed it I told it I would get it a treat later. It sniffed, playing on my sympathies.

Except for the piano, the living room doesn't have any furniture. That's because most furniture is completely untrustworthy. The piano had been with me forever, and it had never given me any trouble, so I let it stay.

I pointed at the floor.

"Sit," I told him.

He hesitated, but obeyed. More grudging respect.

I went to the bathroom and turned off the water, which was still trickling into the tub. The sculptures were all gone now and the water had settled into a boring clump at the bottom of the tub. What a waste.

Back in the living room I stood, arms crossed. "Okay." I said. "You're in. What's your name?"

"Stan Haas," he said.

"All right, Stan. What do you want?"

He looked up at me, very serious. "Ms. Langley, do you understand your arrangement with the hospital?"

"Yeah, sure. The doctor brings me drugs, and the hospital gets money from my short bastard accountant."

"That's about right," he said. "But your arrangement with us is rather unusual. We don't usually contract with a patient for a doctor who will make house calls and deliver drugs to a patient who—"

"Hey," I said, "what is this, song and dance time? We both know what the contract says. Do your job."

"It's not that simple. Medical policies are tightening, and we're re-evaluating all of our psychiatric patients in light of these new policies. If we had you under constant observation, it would be a different matter, but since we don't—"

"Are you going to try to have me declared mentally

incompetent? Better talk to my little brother first. He tried that. He failed."

"No, no." He held his hands up. "I've read the report. You are clearly quite capable of convincing the court of your sanity."

"Oh hell yeah. Now the pills."

"Why?"

"What the fuck kind of question is that?" My fingers curled into claws. They do that when I get frustrated. "Check my files. The pills help me sleep."

"I know what your files say," he said in his doctor voice. "I want to hear it from you. You're supposed to take them as needed. How many do you have left?"

"Don't play games with me, Haas. Marlow was supposed to bring me another bottle last week. He's late. Now you're late."

"All right." He nodded. "Tell you what, I'll bring you your pills tomorrow, first thing, if you give me something now."

"I'm paying you money, you scumbag. You're supposed to respond when I give you money. That's what doctors do. Do your job."

"No," he said.

"No?"

"No. According to Dr. Marlow's records, you don't need more pills for another week, but I'm betting you're just about out. You want them sooner, you cooperate with me."

I crouched down in front of him and looked straight into his eyes, which were almost black, like his hair. I grinned. Now I had him.

"You trying to blackmail me?"

"Only a little. I want a blood sample."

"Blood sample?" That I hadn't expected. I stood up. "I thought you just wanted sex. The one time a doctor did, it wasn't so bad. Tall and quick. Like a blood draw, I guess." I ran my fingers through my hair. "What do you want it for?"

"Analysis of your condition."

"Not interested."

He shrugged. "All right, then," he said. He picked up his doctor-bag and stood. He was taller than me now, which I didn't like. Not taller than her, though, I was pretty sure. "See you in a couple of weeks, Ms. Langley." He walked to the front door. I followed him.

"Hey wait," I said.

"Blood test, Ms. Langley. Yes or no."

He grabbed the door handle. The door screamed. I screamed back at it. I didn't want to stop, so I kept screaming.

Something hurt my shoulders, and I tried to push it away, but it pushed back. The floor always surprises me that way. I opened my eyes and glared into the carpet. Something pulled me onto my feet and someone was making noises and wouldn't let me go.

I guess I stopped screaming for a time, because I started up again.

The door joined in, and after a while I ran out of air. The something let me go and I went back down to hugging the floor. I wanted to cry. Maybe I did.

THE DOOR WOULD NEVER FORGIVE me now, not even for two cookies.

I heard voices.

"I'm her doctor."

"I'm calling the cops," Victor said, in his nasal voice.

I rolled over and looked up. Two dark suits cornered the door, which stood half-opened in a frozen, terrified silence.

"Oh Jesus, Victor", I said to the rat-faced man. "Shut the door. It's been through hell today."

"My God, Susan," he whined, "are you all right? Did he hurt you?"

"You're an idiot. He's taking over for Marlow." I waved my hand in their general direction. "Stan Haas. Victor Biglow. You've met. Now come in and *shut the door*."

"Doctor, eh?" Victor asked as they both stepped in. Victor shut the door. Not nearly gently enough. "What are you doing here, Doctor? A physical exam? Right here on the floor? Very professional."

Victor was suspicious of other people. It was one of his few good qualities.

"She was naked when I came to the door, Mr. Biglow."

"Sure she was. Any harassment complaints on your record yet, doctor?"

The cracks in the ceiling were dancing to the singing in my ears.

"Victor," I said, "why are you here?"

"I have papers for you to sign."

"Hell. Can't you give me some notice?

"How? Got Internet yet, Susan? How about a phone?"

"All right. Bring them here."

I rolled onto my side. Victor tried to pretend not to see my breasts as he stepped closer, squatted down, and opened his paper-box.

I looked inside. Lots of papers. I knew that he knew, because I had already told him, that the papers make babies in the box. That's why there were always so many of them. But he wouldn't do anything about it. They needed operations, I told him. Just like cats.

He reached in and some of the papers followed his hand out. He closed the box, which clicked, and smoothed the papers to lie flat on top. He pushed the box in front of me and handed me his black metal pen.

I started to sign the first one, which was our standard quarterly contract, the one that kept Victor in charge of my finances. I paused.

"A raise? Hell, no, Victor."

"It's the going rate, Susan," he said.

"No, it's not."

"How would you know?" He was carefully not looking at me. "When was the last time you priced accountants, Susan? If you want someone else, you're free to find someone."

I sat up. "You take extra already, Victor, I know you do."

He snatch the papers back.

"Are you calling for an audit, Susan?" He put the papers in his paper-box, clicked it shut and stood. "I'm happy to do that for you. You'll have to come down to my office to oversee it, of course."

That was bad. The outside made me puke, made me dizzy. He knew that. I inhaled to say something, but nothing happened.

"Well? You going to sign the contract or should I let the bills come here to you?"

I hugged my knees. "I pay you a lot already."

"Not enough for this," he said.

Haas broke in with that quiet, reasonable, doctor-voice of his.

"I'll oversee an audit if you want, Ms. Langley."

"This is none of your business," Victor told him. "It's between me and Susan."

"It's my business if Ms. Langley wants it be, Mr. Biglow."

I stood up so fast that my breasts bounced. Victor's eyes went to them and away, which made me smile. I walked up close to him.

"What is it about girl parts that makes you act so weird?" I asked. Victor pretended that I was a door.

"Ms. Langley, do you want me to handle an audit for you?" Haas asked.

"Susan," Victor said, nasal and sincere, "he's a <u>doctor</u>. I can't believe you'd trust him after what you went through with your grandmother."

I grabbed a bit of carpet fuzz with my toes. "Yeah, doc, you can do the audit for me."

"I don't believe this," Victor said angrily. "You don't know what I do for you. You have no clue. Who was it who handled your inheritance when your grandmother passed? Who set up your investments? Who keeps your money-grubbing family at bay? I don't just pay your bills, Susan. I handle it <u>all</u>. And you want me to stop?"

I swallowed. My stomach hurt. He was waiting for me to say something, but my throat had closed up. I shook my head and the walls groaned. I couldn't concentrate.

"Fine," Victor said in a clipped voice. He opened the door and glared at the doctor and then at me. "If you don't trust me, I don't want to work for you. Handle your own money. I'll just tell the creditors where you live, and you can explain to them why you can't pay your own bills, why you don't own a phone, and why your doctor has to make house calls." He shook his head. "You're a nut case, Susan. You ought to be in an institution. I'll send my final bill."

I waved my left breast at him. He left, slamming the door, which sobbed piteously. I winced.

"Shit," I said. "What am I going to do now?"

"Well," Haas said. "How about we start with a blood sample?"

The door was weeping unrestrainedly now. I wouldn't sleep tonight, even with the noise-box all the way on.

"What the hell," I said, and held out my arm.

THE NEXT TIME the doctor came, he offered a fresh benediction from the science gods. One prayer was the same as the next to me, so I gave up my old pills for the new ones. He came by almost every day to remind me to worship and to help me with the papers that kept having litters.

My nights went through the dryer enough times to soften and fade. The sharp-tipped swords of fire that hung down at me from the nighttime heavens became small dots of light that shone through my window.

The doors talked less of rebellion and more about wallpaper.

I still heard her in the basement.

One night my sleep was disturbed by the sound of her steps on the basement stairs. I knew it was her tread on the wood, though I had never heard it before, because it was slow, heavy, and tentative, as though she were uncertain that the wood would support her. The basement door resisted her with the deadbolt. She rattled the knob for long minutes and was silent.

I must have fallen asleep again, because the loud banging sound ripped me fully awake. I realized with a shock that the basement no longer held, confined, or restrained her.

Her feet made small sounds as they shuffled the hallway toward my room. I heard carpet tear as the nails that made up her boots caught and she pulled loose. I huddled under the blankets.

I was careful. My door was locked, too, murmuring sleepily of flowers. She rattled the knob. I burrowed under the pillow.

For a moment there was silence. Then she kicked in the door.

I held my breath and pretended I was a wall.

"I want to talk to you," she said. Her a voice sounded like a whirlwind that had been forced through a plastic straw.

I was suddenly, deeply remorseful that I had not put up more wallpaper.

She kicked my bed lightly a few times, presumably to get my attention. She had it. I whimpered.

"I want to talk to you," she repeated.

"I'm sorry about the nails," I cried into the blankets, "I didn't think you'd mind."

"I want to talk to you," she said again.

I yanked the covers off my face.

She stood tall, my golden-haired amazon, as perfect as could be, clothed only in the metal dressings I had so laboriously given her, so often.

Her blue eyes, which never moved, were locked on mine.

"Talk to me, or I'll break you," she said.

I sat up in bed, blankets around my shoulders, back to the wall.

"What do you want?" I whispered.

"I want to know why you take the pills," she said, crossing her arms. "The ones that change you. Why do you take them?"

"My accountant quit."

"Oh." She nodded. She squatted, examining a loose nail on her leg.

"So it's that or find another accountant," I explained.

She pulled the nail out and tossed it aside.

"When you take the pills, you change things." She lifted one foot and balanced on the other, holding her arms straight out to the side, birdlike.

"I do?"

"Yes. And you don't come downstairs anymore, like you used to."

"I didn't think you'd notice," I mumbled.

"You didn't think I noticed you hammering nails into me?" Her hands went to her hips.

"I hoped you wouldn't. Didn't want you mad at me."

She threw her arms out to the side, kicked, and turned like a dancer, ending on both feet. "I'm not mad. I'm changing."

"Oh," I said, feeling uncertain. "Is that good?"

"If you keep taking the pills, you'll change everything. You know that, don't you?"

"Yeah."

I had known, about the changing, I just hadn't known that I had. Now I knew that I knew.

"You are already changing me," she said, looking at me. She stood up straight, let her hands fall to her sides.

"How?" I asked. "How am I changing you?"

She didn't reply. I watched her eyes, but they had gone still. I waited for her to say something.

It had been weeks since I named her, so I wasn't sure what to call her now. I spoke the names I remembered. She didn't respond.

I waited, waited some more, then stood, tentatively reaching out my hand to touch her. Cold. Hard. I tried to pick her up, but she was too heavy. I didn't know what else to do, so I lowered her to the floor and put my blanket over her. Eventually I went back to bed.

When I woke late morning, she was gone.

***

"A CORRECTABLE CONDITION."

The world swam in white and brown bitter stink as I bent over the toilet. I threw up again.

Correctable.

I pulled the handle. It all mixed and went down and away. I flushed again and sat on the cool tiles.

"Side effects," he had said.

"Side effects?" I had asked. "What kind of side effects?"

"Dizziness, nausea. Mild in most people. You probably won't notice a thing."

"Ha." I said to the toilet.

"You okay, Susie?"

"Yes." He would be here in a few minutes, according to the clock I could just see from the bathroom. The one I had bought, out there in the world. With money. My money. Made me feel civilized, that clock on the coffee table. Tick tick. Super civilized.

If I could do that, I could do anything.

"Come on, sweetheart. Put floor under your feet and you'll feel better. Doc'll be here soon."

I grabbed the sides of the sink and pulled myself up. I washed my face and rinsed my mouth and looked myself over in the mirror. Two eyes, a mouth, and a nose. All in place. Not bad, considering. I went to the clock.

"There you go. Marvelous. Ready?"

"Better be."

The doorbell rang. I went to the door. He waved through the glass. I let him in.

"Good morning, Ms. Langley," he said, reaching down to the pile of mail that had come through the slot and handing it to me.

"Thanks." I glanced at them. "Bills," I said, feeling a mix of terror and elation. "I did the last bunch," I told him. "Only a bit of help. Fed them to the mailbox at the corner. Just like a real person."

"You are doing well. How do you feel?"

"Not bad, other than puking my guts out."

"Nausea, still?" We walked into the living room together.

He dug into his doctor bag and pulled out a small bottle of pills. "That should stop as soon as your body adjusts to the medication, and—"

We had been sitting on the sofa with coffee and the morning paper when I had run to the bathroom. She was sitting still now, holding a section of the paper open on her knees.

Some of his fingers opened around the bottle in his hand and pointed toward her. "Who—" he hesitated, stared, opened his mouth again, stopped.

"Oh," I said, feeling awkward. "Ah. This is—"

Who was she today?. "Nancy," I said, pretty sure that was right. "My very good friend, Nancy. She lives… downstairs."

He didn't say anything, but his face showed concern tinged with suspicion. Wanted to know what the deal was. He was a know-the-deal kind of guy.

His face had gone very still.

"Doctor?"

Nancy laughed softly.

I touched his arm. It was hard.

"Okay, that's not good," I said.

She waved a hand. "He'll be fine." She took a sip of coffee, her big blue eyes on me. "You don't worry when I do that, right?"

"Well, no, but you started that way." I handed her the bundle of mail, my eyes still on him.

"Pills," she reminded.

I gently disengaged the bottle from his half-open fingers, making sure not to disturb his balance. I put the bottle in front of her.

"Look, it's got my name on it. How cool is that?"

Nancy smiled. Amused. Tolerant. Just like a real person.

"Okay, this one—" she held up an envelope. "That's electricity. We need that."

"Lights and stuff." I glanced at him. He was still unmoving. "Did you do that to him? Did I?"

She opened another envelope.

"Sometimes it's hard to be sure," she said. "When I go downstairs, I suspect he'll come around."

"Will he remember?"

She shrugged. "I bet he'll manage not to, you know?"

I could understand that. I thought about the last year. Remembering wasn't everything it was cracked up to be. I looked at Nancy. Looked at the bottle of pills.

"Too bad he couldn't stay awake."

"We do what we can with the tools we've got. Pass me the checkbook, would you?"

The checks were blue and green, with faint, bulbous orange fish all over them. When we got them I made sure my name was on every one.

"Your gramma would be proud."

"Do you think so?"

"She would be, Susie."

She scribbled, filling out the numbers and names and the other stuff. I rocked, eager for my turn.

"Remember to thank Doctor Haas when he's back."

"I will."

"All right, All right. Stop bouncing. Here." She handed me the pen and the checkbook. "Try to make each scrawl look like the rest, okay?"

"Okay."

I put the checkbook on the table took a deep breath and on the signature line drew four circles and some whiskers. Looked almost like a bunny. We do what we can with the tools we've got.

I was getting better all the time.

"Really, Susie," Nancy said, teasingly. But she smiled. I could tell that she understood.

MIRROR TEST

In 2011, Intel Corporation put out a call for science fiction that explored the future of some of Intel's then-current research and development.

I combined virtual reality, machine learning, and facial recognition to explore what happens when software can tell intimate things about what we humans are thinking.

Other than Cory Doctorow's spotlight story, all submitted stories were blind-juried. That is, evaluated without any identifying information. Five stories were selected for the fiction part of the anthology, and mine was one of them.

The technology in this story is still very much in our future.

Also in our future is a tech industry that treats women as well as it does men. When I was an engineer last century, I was confident that we'd be there by now. We're not.

The main character in "Mirror Test," Marguerite Allohay, has just had a very promising interview with a tech company.

The question is: does she want the job enough to pass the test?

First published in *The Tomorrow Project Anthology—Seattle*, Intel Corporation, 2011.

MARGUERITE ALLOHAY BOARDED the South Lake Union Transit train, followed by snickering tourists who had just worked out the acronym. She slid into a window seat and stared out at a suddenly overcast Seattle. Hadn't it been sunny just a bit ago, on her walk to the train? That must have been summer, right there. An old joke but still somehow grimly hilarious to sun-starved Seattle natives.

It was the final leg of her trip from Redmond via light rail from ULearnIT—you'd think they could afford a decent name—where she had just finished her second and perhaps final interview.

It had, to all appearances, gone well. Well enough that, baring a few details, she might even make their short list.

Passing the Tesla dealership she remembered a webcast about a women's version, not pink but mauve and cheap enough that someone like her could afford it if she never ever wanted to own a home. For a moment she imagined walking in, zeroing out her credit and driving off into the sunset. Or, given this wretched overcast, into the slowly darkening gloom. Just putting this whole silly job idea out of her head.

Details. Wasn't that where the devil lived?

—

MARGUERITE THUMBED the front door lock. She felt smug every time she saw other people fumbling for house keys and now she struggled to hang onto that sense of smug as she stepped inside but the interview kept coming back.

Her degrees in psychology and computer science had led her to this interview as surely as—well, as surely as the unpracticed arrow misses the mark a whole bunch of times before it finds a target. She'd stumbled around for years doing this and that. Now she had a seriously good chance at working in collaborative learning doing cutting edge work for a well-funded company. It was a target worth aiming at.

As a "Facilitator." Because teachers, Richard Ruhland, ULearnIT CEO, had assured her, were on the way out.

"Thing of the past, Margret" said Ruhland. He laughed as if putting teachers in the past were his own personal triumph.

It put her on edge, his laugh, along with the way he kept forgetting her name. She also wanted to challenge him on his statement about teachers. But she wanted the job more.

"Well, that should save you a lot of money," she said, intending to be clever.

"Yes, exactly, Margret," he answered without a trace of humor. "But more importantly it's effective. Because our students work collaboratively—and by that I mean creatively—with the subject matter, they end up teaching each other and learning more effectively. Turns out that our learning approach is 87.2 percent more effective than even the best of traditional university level courses. Better comprehension, better retention. Eighty-seven point two. Can you believe that?"

She nodded slowly. She'd read ULearnIT's white paper. While she had some misgivings about their methodology and statistical rigor, it was clear they had something interesting. Interesting enough that she'd canceled another interview at the U-Dub to be here today.

Get the job first, she told herself, argue later.

"It's Marguerite," she found herself saying.

"What?"

"My name. Marguerite."

"Ah. 'Marge' okay, then?"

"Sure," she said, suppressing a wince. "Tell me about the facilitator position?"

"We need someone in the VR along with the students

who can guide their activities and perceptions. You know about recent phobia alleviation and PTSD therapies using VR?"

Somewhat, she wanted to say. But that was where women always went wrong in these sorts of interviews. Underplaying their strengths. A man would just say yes.

"Yes," she said.

"Well, that's all wrong." He waved his hand as if to erase this entire arm of progressive psychological approaches. "They spend too much time getting the subject to say how they feel and what the issue is. We don't need the subject to tell us anything—we listen with biometrics. Get the data direct."

"I see," she said, not sure she did.

"Turns out micro-expression recognition—MER—is the magic sauce. Pretty damned accurate, if you have a system that learns from the user. You have any idea how much people give away in micromovements, if you have the eyes to see it?"

She nodded, trying to keep her expression neutral.

"Our MER analysis is so good we've patented it. Our system, which we call CHEMERA, learns the person behind the face."

"And how does that connect to learning?"

"You're familiar with Fagan's Friction Reduction thesis?"

She'd read the paper, though she hoped he wouldn't pump her for details. He went on with barely a pause.

"Fagan says that to the degree you can get input devices out of the way of a computer-mediated interaction—dispense with keyboards, mice, gestures—all that intermediary motion—you don't compete with the essential cognitive learning process. We call it frictionless learning."

"You don't use any input devices at all?"

"Don't need 'em. CHEMERA creates a collaborative VR

based on MER analysis and biometrics. Between our frictionless learning and the social motive force of collaboration—you know, peer-pressure—we get stellar results in both absorption and retention. There's never been anything like this, not at any university, not at any industrial R&D silo. We're changing the science of teaching and revolutionizing a thousand years of pedagogy. Margret, you want in on this?"

"Yes," she found herself saying. She had thought she was immune to such sales tactics, but clearly not. He knew how to sell, all right. The board knew what they were doing when they pulled him to be CEO.

"Glad to hear it. Frankly, I think you're just what we need."

A thrill went through her. She could, if she played her cards just right, have this job.

"Tell me more about what the facilitator does."

"As I said, teachers are now redundant. But having someone in the VR who can steer student attention toward the material is essential. It turns out that the best way to teach is to let students play with real world objects in CHEMERA's lucid-dream-logic VR. So, for example, a database as a building, rows as floors, records as rooms. Right? Classic model."

She nodded.

"But that breaks down fast when you throw in complicated queries and interconnected data structures. So the model has to be flexible. Maybe it needs to be a building over here and an anthill over there. And an espresso machine. It's going to be collaborative, creative, and personal. That's where you come in."

"Anthills and espresso machines."

"Exactly. You've got doctorates in Computer Science and Psychology."

"Dissertations pending."

He waved a hand to dismiss her caveat. "Your job is to help steer the students toward the models most appropriate to the material. Usually students do just fine with a little nudge here and there, or so our initial experience indicates. It's collaboration, after all. But you'll have a stronger input. A majority vote, if you will."

"I see," she said.

"But you're also there to keep them from going astray. You might be surprised at what people reveal once you stop distracting them with the hand-eye coordination requirements that traditional input devices require." Ruhland leaned forward. "Tell me, Marge: what do most people think about most of the time?"

"Sex," she replied unhesitatingly. Or food, she didn't say. Or what others think of them. But from his expression and body language, it was obvious what answer he wanted.

"Exactly. So your job is to watch over them, keep them from doing things in the VR they don't really want to do. Sure, we could modify the engine to prevent those things from even arising, but we've discovered that means throwing out the baby with the bathwater. People who aren't allowed free reign with their expression don't, well—express. So we need someone there to help guide their creations a bit."

It made sense. This was something sensitive parents and teachers had known forever but academia was just catching on to. If you didn't let people talk about what was on their mind, the way they talked about anything else at all was constrained by what they weren't allowed to say.

"So my job would be to guide student exploration toward the lesson plan. To keep it away from less relevant subjects."

"Exactly. To be the mature presence. The adult, if you will."

"I see," she said. Then, summoning confidence she wasn't quite sure she felt, she said, "I'm who you want, then. I've got the relevant experience. I can do this."

He twitched his eyebrows up once and looked down at the stack of papers before him, which included her resume, thesis proposals on learning models in computer science, and a few glowing letters of recommendation.

"You're a strong candidate, no question. You'll be on our short list if the reflective self-assessment goes well."

"The what?"

"Ah yes. Let me get you a consent and release form."

SHE PUSHED the front door shut behind her with a heel.

"I'm home," she called.

The sound of a chair moving across wood floor on casters was followed by Bert's ginger colored head popping out from behind a door at sitting height. "Hey there." He disappeared a moment, and walked into the room, smiling. "How did it go?"

"Mr. CEO-guy says I could be on the short list."

"Well, well. Let's celebrate." He opened a cabinet. "Red or white?"

"Red."

He poured two glasses of Shiraz and handed her one. "To your future at—what is that name again?

"ULearnIT. Yeah, I know. Sounds like a mini-mart."

"It does." He handed her a glass.

"But. I'm not counting chickens just yet."

"You'll get it. You're brilliant." He held up his glass and she reluctantly clinked it with her own. While he sipped she stared down into the thick red depths of her wine.

No doubt she was overreacting. Their system wasn't going to read her mind. Pupil dilation, eye-tracking, heart-rate and so forth—that it would read. But no matter how good ULearnIT's micro-expression recognition analysis might be, her own thoughts were still going to be hers. Private.

A collaborative VR where students could be distracted by whatever they were really thinking who therefore needed adult supervision? It sure sounded like mind-reading.

She reached across the table for a napkin and knocked her wine glass over, splattering Bert, the table, the floor.

"Hell," she said, standing. Bert went to the kitchen, came back with a bottle of white wine and a towel. He poured white wine onto the carpet on top of the red.

"Do you know what you're doing?" she asked.

He grinned. "Yep." He knelt down, dabbed the wet mess on the carpet. "Just like you do, babe. So I'm sensing some hesitation here. The interview went well?"

"I don't know. Maybe not."

He stood, looked at her thoughtfully.

"I should have picked white," she said.

"It's just a carpet. What happened?"

"They want me to take a self-assessment test."

"So?" He refilled her glass with red wine.

"You sure you want to take the risk?"

He grinned, wadded up the soaked rag and put it on the table. "No risk, no reward, I always say. So why are you worried?"

She sighed, started to speak, stopped herself. "How can you tell I'm worried?"

"Well—" he took a sip, gestured at her with his wine glass. "It's just the way you come across."

"Right. Humans are really good at picking up subtle information about each other. A lot of it has to do with tone and nearly invisible, unconscious facial expressions, called micro-expressions. On top of that, you've learned me. You're an expert on me. I think this is what ULearnIT's done, only they do it very fast."

"Okay, I could be impressed."

"Yes. I won't know until I try it, but—yes. They're using facial analysis. Biometrics like blood pressure, heart rate, skin galvanization. Voice analysis. Your body becomes the input device."

"Game companies already do that, no?"

She shook her head. "This is way beyond conscious intentional gestures into the unconscious and involuntary ones. Micro-expression analysis is their breakthrough tech. Their system analyzes and optimizes for each user, keys in on the individual's particular presentation."

"And what do they want you for?"

"Baby sitter."

He laughed. "Really?"

"Sort of. The students collaborate on a subject's lesson plan. Data structures, for example. Maybe they imagine brightly colored blocks as code snippets and there they are, presto, all around them in the VR. They can create whatever they want. Someone has to keep them from having too much fun."

"You."

"Maybe."

"You're good at tests."

"It's not that kind of test."

"I don't get it."

"Look, the system tunes itself to each person. Like someone who listens really, really well. Like you do."

He gave her an aw-shucks look and put his hand on hers. "That sounds like a good thing. Less confusion, right?"

"Less privacy. Anyone can see what you're thinking."

"Ah."

"So they want to know if my self-image is healthy enough to guide a classroom of students away from thinking about sex and toward thinking about computers."

"Your self-image is as healthy as anyone's I know, Reet."

She picked up the wine soaked rag and considered it for a moment.

"They aren't looking for someone with two doctorates. They're looking for someone with mental and emotional ballast. Am I that someone?"

"Of course you are."

She sighed. "How would you feel if a job you really wanted depended on a mind-reading computer's analysis of what you thought of yourself?"

SHE STRUGGLED with what to wear to the test, realizing the absurdity of it even as she did. She settled for conservative: black pants and a beige top, a light brown jacket. Staring at herself in the mirror, she wondered if the other applicants taking this test were this nervous. And dressing in front of a mirror. Probably not.

At ULearnIT, she was shown to the labs. A cheerful woman with close cropped pale hair greeted her at the door.

"Hi, Ms. Allohay, I'm Sal. I'll be your tech today. Please take a seat." Sal gestured at a chair that looked entirely too much like a dentist's chair.

She sat down, exhaled slowly.

Sal reached up and swiveled over Marguerite's head and a device that looked quite a bit like an x-ray machine.

"And have you been flossing regularly?," Sal asked. Seeing Marguerite's expression, she added "Sorry. Sometimes I think I'm funny when I'm not."

"No, no, it's fine."

"Anyway, there's nothing to worry about. It's completely non-intrusive. No x-rays or anything. The system is just, well. Observing."

Just. Right.

"This is the camera I'm positioning now. And if you would put this headset on...? The built-in goggles and earphones should fit so comfortably you can hardly tell they're there—that's what the marketing glossy says. Ha. After a few hours, you'll notice them." She grinned. "Comfortable enough for now?"

"Yes."

"Okay, now this goes on your hand. Heart rate, blood pressure, GSR and so on. Good?"

"Yes."

"I know you've talked to Mr. Ruhland about how the systems works, but most people find it a little surprising, how responsive the system is. You'll see some flickering at first— that's the subliminal stroboscopic initialization—and hear some odd sounds, too. That's CHEMERA's way of calibrating your expressions with what it knows about people like you."

"People like me?"

"I mean that in the demographic sense. Gender, age, place of origin. CHEMERA even catches accent tones and compares against its stored sample knowledge base to have an idea what you might be like, what you might prefer."

What she'd prefer is to be somewhere else, she didn't say.

"You know a lot about this system."

"I'm an intern, but when I grow up, I hope to be a facilitator, like you."

"Not there yet. I have to pass this test first. Any advice?"

Sal smiled a bit, wrapped a soft band around Marguerite's wrist to secure the device. "Try to relax."

Standard advice for stress-producing psych tests. Intended to be reassuring but not.

"Okay, you're all hooked up. I'll start up CHEMERA. Once you're in the VR, you'll notice is a door. Then just think about opening the door, and keep thinking about it until it opens. That's our basic check that CHEMERA is reading you. Then go into the room. That tells us you're ready to start the test."

She'd done pretty well at tests in the past, both the required exams and the multitude of self-evaluation tests that a Ph.D. in psychology trailed in its wake, but this was the first time she'd had a computer judging her—well, her character. That's what this was, really.

And she didn't like it. The problem wasn't what she thought of herself, but what the system thought she thought of herself. She was, she realized, feeling slightly queasy.

A door appeared in front of her. Simple, grey, with a knob. As directed, she thought about opening the door, and as she did, she moved closer to the door. A hand extended from her point-of-view and turned the knob. It opened and she stepped through.

Sal was right: even with the explanation, she was stunned. No joystick, no mouse, no keyboard—not even voice commands. Nothing but her intent, reflected in the subtlest movements of her face, eyes, probably skin, heart rate, breath.

It was learning her, just as Ruhland said. "Fast" was an understatement.

She had entered a small room. The room's simple lines moved slightly as they would if she were walking. Sal's avatar —a cartoonish woman with short-cropped pale hair— appeared next to her.

"Welcome to CHEMERA!" Sal said cheerfully. "Here are the instructions I'm required to read to you once you're here.

You've already signed a consent and release, so you know we may record this session. Safety is, of course, our first concern. If at any time you want to stop the test, just say "stop". We reserve the right to terminate the test at any time if it in our sole discretion we believe there is any risk to you. Do you understand and agree to these terms?"

This wasn't helping her to be calm, not a bit.

"Yes."

A mirror appeared in front of Marguerite. An image appeared in the mirror, but so briefly she could barely see that it looked like a bit like her. The image flickered, details of color and shape changing too fast for her to follow.

Suddenly it settled. In the frame of the mirror was Marguerite's avatar. It looked as much like her as they usually did: brownish red hair in a pixie cut, dressed in sensible browns and blacks.

She was impressed. CEMEMRA had just read her physical responses to a series of proposed images, determining what she wanted to see just by watching her reactions.

"Wow," she said.

"Now, all you need to do for this test," Sal said in her headset, "is watch yourself in the mirror. Ready? Good luck!"

Sal's avatar vanished. Marguerite was alone in the room. From the mirror her avatar looked back with big eyes. It was cuter that she was, in the way of avatars, with clear, cartoonish skin, a sharp nose, and wide green eyes.

At this thought it began to change again, slowly enough that she could see the metamorphosis. Her nose broadened slightly, her eyes shrank to more realistic proportions.

Now the face in the mirror was frowning, looking annoyed and unhappy. Her reflection's skin began to blotch. Her hair frizzled out a bit. Her ears grew. In moments she was looking at a version of herself that was distinctly unpleasant. It wasn't wrong, exactly, any more than the cartoonish cute avatar had been, but she was pretty sure she wasn't quite this ugly. She glanced away.

"Marguerite, please look at the mirror. It's only requirement of the test. Thanks so much!"

Marguerite looked back, expecting the wretched caricature, but her original avatar had returned. Cleaning the slate, they called it in psych terminology. People performed better when they knew they could start over. It was something game companies had known for years.

Focus, she told herself sternly. You have to show them you're not a mess. You're a competent woman. You've nearly got a double Ph.D. You're married to an attractive architect. And your face isn't at all blotchy or mousy.

The image in the mirror shifted. A very sad, large nosed, blotchy faced rat-like woman stared back at her. The expression of the rat-like, trollish creature in the mirror went to shock, correctly mirroring the way she felt on seeing it, tiny green eyes widening, ruddy brown hair sticking out at angles around her head.

She had to get a grip. Never mind proving competence, she had to get out of troll-land. Tall, she told herself sternly. Or at least average. And not this ugly. Were those bumps on her face?

Sound came, a slightly unpleasant warbling that stopped suddenly. Into the following silence spoke a voice. A familiar voice.

"All these problems are not going to just take care of themselves. Are they, Marguerite."

She caught her breath in shock. How on earth could CHEMERA generate this, her mother's voice, simply by watching her expressions? How?

Because it was trying things out in a tight loop, seeing how she unconsciously responded, and doing it all so fast that she wasn't even aware of it. It was a complicated, subtle biofeedback device. Her mind raced. This was hard stuff, but CHEMERA was doing it: learning her from subtle inputs and stochastic models, pulling from the recesses of her mind her own mother's voice—a voice she had not heard in over 10 years, not since her mother had died, and had frankly hoped never to hear again.

"Marguerite," her mother's voice came at her, harsh, teasing the syllables of her name apart. "Are you listening to me?"

"Yes," she answered. Why had she answered?

In the mirror her mousy reflection broadened, the hair matting, the face sagging.

"Your problems just won't, no matter how much we pretend, take care of themselves. Will they." The voice twisted inside her like a knife. "Will they."

Surely she had never looked like this. Her slender figure was replaced by a sagging, troll-like monster, with pimples and red blotches.

"I'm sorry, Ms. Allohay," Sals' voice broke through apologetically, "but you'll have to open your eyes."

"Okay," Marguerite mumbled. She forced herself to look at creature before her, dressed in appalling beige frills.

"Marguerite," her mother's voice hissed. "No one can help you if you don't listen."

She would simply have to imagine it away. What did she look like? Slender. Adult. She never wore this stuff any more, never ever—

God, what if the tech could hear this? Was this all being recorded? Of course it was.

They're trying to figure out if you're an adult enough to sit in this VR with a dozen professionals and guide them away from creating pornographic videos. Good thing you've got such a solid grasp on your own self-image.

She exhaled slowly, completely, letting her lungs refill slowly. All right, never mind how she looked. How did she feel? Shaken, is how she felt, but beyond that? Beyond that, somewhere, was a place of acceptance of herself, flaws and all, something her mother had never given her so couldn't take from her.

"Ms. Allohay—"

"Yes, sorry." She opened her eyes again.

The mirror was empty. She blinked. Empty? She wasn't even there?

Another painfully familiar voice came to her.

"Hello?"

"Daddy?" came the reply. Her own voice, damnit. How the hell—

"Who?" her father's voice asked, with clear amusement.

"It's Marguerite!" she heard herself say, tearfully. She remembered the feel of the phone, tight against her ear. How old had she been? Six? Seven?

"I don't know any Marguerite. You must have a wrong number."

"Daddy, please."

Eyes on the mirror, she reminded herself. She had looked away too often already. But it was still empty. It reflected a room, but she wasn't in it.

"Well, now," her father's voice drawled, "it does seem to me that I used to have another daughter, but she wouldn't stay where she was put. Off wandering. Suppose the faeries must have took her."

"Daddy, I went to look at the pet store. I was only gone a minute. Please! Come get me."

"Ah, too many children to feed anyway. Hope the faeries take good care of her!"

"Daddy, no!"

Click.

Click? Had he really done that, just hung up on her? Surely not. But in memory, he had. Cut her off, just like that. Tossed her aside, forgotten her, and she was—nothing.

And so the empty mirror. There were, after all, some things worse than a poor self-image.

She felt raw. She craved coffee. How very Seattle of her. She promised herself a triple cap when this was all over.

And when they looked at this recording, what would they see?

Mommy and daddy issues. How cliché. A woman with body and self-esteem issues. How classic.

But everyone has issues, right?

She again forced herself to regular breathing, to recall the sunlight on her face from this morning, a few minutes before she'd walked into the building. The warmth, the light. A different world. The real one.

If she couldn't show control here all by herself, how could they trust her with students? How much worse would this be when there were others in here with her? She was supposed to be the one who kept the teaching sessions oriented on the lessons, kept the students learning. Be the rudder that kept the boat from capsizing.

How long was this damned test, anyway?

A shape was forming in the mirror. Dread pooled in her stomach.

"Uh, Ms. Allohay? I'm monitoring your vitals and your heart rate and blood pressure are in the orange. Do you want to stop the test?"

"No!"

She'd probably already failed, but if she exited now, it'd be a sure thing.

"Okay! Just say the word."

She knew the word. She had no intention of saying it.

In the mirror her avatar looked scared and angry, which

made sense. But also in the mirror, her avatar wasn't alone. Around her were—the students? Must be. Eager looking students. Staring at her avatar, eyes wide, hands reaching. Toward her.

Oh hell. This was exactly what she couldn't let happen.

"No," she said determinedly, but her reflection in the mirror said nothing. Her avatar was beginning to smile, actually, to move around a bit and—she was wriggling, is what she was doing. Wriggling under the touch of many petting, groping hands. The hands seemed to multiply, arms stretching from the edges of the mirror around the closely gathered men—and was that a woman, too?—standing near her. Caressing. Reaching under her clothes.

A certain, unmistakable sound started to come from her avatar. <u>Oh Christ.</u>

Thinking of her watchers, she felt sick. This was not in her head, couldn't be. Was it part of the test to throw this kind of filth at her to see what she would do?

With a word she could make it all end. Maybe she should bail before it got worse. Nothing wrong with a position in research or database administration. Did she really need this job?

Her avatar was clearly having a better and better time, making classic female sexual vocalizations. At least someone was having fun here. If only no one were watching, she found herself thinking, this might not be so bad...

Ah, so that's what was going on. At the surface she was repulsed—or thought she was—but under that was classic, simple desire and thus this creation of these overly friendly hands.

And if this was her creation, those were her hands. They belonged to her, not anyone else. And that meant—well. That meant she could tell them them—not with the anger or denial that made them more persistent—to cut it out.

Her reflection was getting very into this. One hand started pulling up her skirt. No, no, this wasn't what she wanted to do—or rather, to demonstrate herself doing.

But, she knew, her unconscious mind wouldn't respond to negatives. She needed something positive. These hands needed to grab something else. Database records, perhaps? No, too abstract. Something vivid, visual. Immediate. Compelling. At least to her, to the parts of her that were creating this.

Since she was a bundle of clichés anyway, how much further could she go?

Kittens.

Adorable, astounded, delighted, playful kittens. One in every hand, with a few extra hands dangling strings. Strings as pointers. The underlying data structure, represented by hands and strings and kittens. There—not just cute, but relevant cute, too! And while she was at it, a black mother cat happily curled and purring in her avatar's arms.

She heard the purr as the cat appeared in her arms. Kittens were suddenly everywhere—black, orange, white, calico—held and played with by all these hands, tussling with each other on the floor. One was even perched on a student's shoulder, watching the proceedings with feline fascination. A small tuxedo kitty on the floor batted insistently at the hem of her dress. Her avatar's smile had turned amused.

So that's how it worked here. Where you put your focus was what CHEMERA made for you. Avoidance and denial were just invitations to make manifest what you didn't want to see.

It wasn't that sex wasn't a good idea, she reflected, finally beginning to warm to this process, but that sometimes kittens were a little more to the point.

THE NEXT DAY went by without a word from Ruhland or anyone at ULearnIT, then another, and if she let herself start to think about what she'd done in CHEMERA she could feel herself regretting the whole thing.

Maybe they didn't want someone with her particular issues. Maybe there really were people out there who didn't have these things in their heads, didn't have these issues. Maybe there was someone who could handle themselves in the VR better. It was possible that she simply didn't get the job.

Back at ULearnIT, someone—probably Ruhland—was reviewing a recording of her most vulnerable feelings made manifest, to see if she was a suitable guide for a classroom of engineers and IT specialists. It wasn't a comforting thought.

She almost hoped she'd never hear back from them when Ruhland called. His image smiled at her from her screen.

"Kittens? Well, well. Cute."

She felt herself blush, and then felt annoyed.

"Thank you. I think. Do you want me for the position or don't you?"

"Yes, we do, Marge."

"Marguerite."

"What?"

"My name. Marguerite. When you know me better, you can call me 'Reet', but for now, I want all three syllables."

He hesitated a moment. "All right. Marguerite it is."

"So I passed the test, then?"

"It's not really pass-fail. It's more about seeing what you do when you're there. You'd be surprised at how many people don't finish it at all."

"Really."

He chuckled. "You'd think it was hard to stand there and look in a mirror."

"Have you taken it?"

He blinked. "Congratulations, Marguerite, and welcome to the team. You'll have an offer in your inbox by the end of day."

"Thank you."

"Kittens," Ruhland said again, shaking his head, smiling. "I didn't see that coming."

"Kittens love mirrors," Marguerite said. "They always wonder who that other kitty is behind the glass."

Ruhland nodded thoughtfully. "I suppose they do."

SEEKING THE SINGULARITY

Wikipedia, the 21st century's extravagantly cluttered apology for the vanished Britannica offers a multitude of definitions for this, perhaps the defining (in its lack of clear definition) proposal of the post-quantum age. Quantum theory plays into this powerfully: the multiplex universe, the intermixture of design and coincidence, the conflation of Schrodinger's Cat, dead and alive and there is no more discipline or finality in that cascade of definition than there is of the increasingly confused universe. The most salient—at least in computer tech and in heavy industry—is that the Singularity represents that point at which the devices themselves have ascendant, sealed the deal, become uncontrollable. Their unwitting creators, with much deliberation (and then again with none at all) have given primacy to a circumstance beyond their ability to manipulate.

That is the most or at least more common definition and was embedded of course within Gernsback-originated science fiction from its beginning close to a century in the past and we are dealing with some of its consequences as I speak; another definition has to do with that multiplex, that conjoinment of immeasurable alternative with inevitable doom and works as separated in time and ideology as *Neuromancer* or its ancestor "The Machine Stops" clearly exemplify. In the storm of event, recursion, controversy, decadence and viciously competing conception the inevitable array of observers, opponents, prophets of sequentiality have all had their go at the emerging circumstances (described by some as "the current unpleasantness") and the projections, extrapolations, commentaries have skewed from left to right, from fascist to libertarian, tending as such polarity often does to meet in the middle. A multiplex universe, a scattering infinity of possibilities can converge to a single nullification just as lust and asepsis (neatly detailed in communiques from NASA) can become indistinguishable.

All a tortuous way of approaching the fictions of Ms. Lyris, engineer and prophet, Sonia of the Singularity who is perhaps the most original, the most gnomic and the most sheer representative of those writers who in this age of Virtual Reality have come to dominate the shrinking cavern in which the true science fiction writers, the descendants and inheritors of John Campbell's Golden age have come to shuddering perch. Her work is extraordinary and ungiving in its flourishes and template…the stories here jingle and jangle and set off rockets which fall back to burn the page. She has explored the audacious (and certainly quantum-generated) possibility that the virtual and the real are indistinguishable, that they merge, that all possibilities conjoin, that our own selves are an accumulation, possibly random, of all our possibilities.

Maureen McHugh about a quarter of a century ago in her properly entitled short story "Virtual Love," a cool investigation of romance among the impossibles, might not have known the full implication of that to which she had opened a door; Gibson's sky which looked like a dead television channel might to him have only been a metaphor for the truncation of possibility, but those pioneers knew not what they had wrought and in time, through the decades, took an implacable and daring observer like Sonia of the Singularity to coolly investigate this; she did it with phantoms and rabbits, betrayers of the true creed locked to its perpetrators; her stories—like these terrible times—are both in and out of possibility and manifest a stunning credibility. She is a writer of shocking prescience whose work—a comparison which presented immediately—is the equivalent of the Beethoven Opus 130 quartets…they are so far ahead of the standards and practices of contemporary criticism that the protocol and language has not yet evolved to fully come to terms. Like Beethoven's Grosse Fugue, worshipped by a few quartet players and barely known to the Philharmonic subscribers, she may be doomed to always be far; two centuries from now still two centuries ahead. But this is a powerful visionary. Too modest—this is one of the faces of quantum—to dare to embrace but I embrace it for her. She is a writer of great significance. Bach and Schubert lay in the ground for decades until Mendelssohn and Arthur Sullivan respectively found them. Let she be the more advantaged.

June 2022/New Jersey
Barry N. Malzberg

ALSO BY

"Big Top," *Space Opera Digest 2020: Have ship, will travel*

The Seer Saga, an immersive high fantasy series

"Not Go Quietly," *Small Gods*

"When Strangers Meet," *Dispatches from Anarres, tales in tribute to Ursula K. Le Guin*

It Might be Sunlight

ABOUT THE AUTHOR

Sonia Orin Lyris's stories have been published in various places, including *Asimov's SF Magazine*, *Wizards of the Coast* anthologies, and *Uncle John's Bathroom Reader*.

Her stories have been called "immersive," "ruthless," and "unsparing."

She is the author of *The Seer Saga*, an epic high-fantasy series, and co-creator of *Rochi*, a divination and gambling game from Campaign Coins.

Her hobbies include dance, martial arts, decoding reality, fine chocolate, humans, and feline poetry.

She loves to hear from readers. Drop a note: https://lyris.org/contact/

A message from the author

If you like this collection, please consider giving it a rating. Same for any book and author: if you like the work, please say so. A note, a good review—these things can make a difference.

Want more?

Follow me on Patreon for juicy updates. Or subscribe for confessional posts and cat pictures.

For straight-up publication news, check my Facebook feed or twitter.

My newsletter is very infrequent but excellently informative. Sign up here. https://lyris.org/subscribe/

My newest published works, all in one place. https://lyris.org/newly-published/

More at my website. https://lyris.org/

facebook.com/authorlyris

twitter.com/slyris

patreon.com/lyris